WITHIN THAT ROOM!

Vera's eccentric Uncle Cyrus dies, leaving her his home — an old castle in Surrey — in his will. Having never seen the place, she decides to go and spend a few days there to decide what to do with it. On arrival at the local railway station, Vera learns that the castle is believed to be haunted. The housekeepers at the castle confirm this and urge her to sell it. Then Vera discovers that one of the rooms is always kept locked because it contains an evil presence. But she is determined to find out what is in there . . .

JOHN RUSSELL FEARN

---------------- ◆ ----------------

WITHIN
THAT
ROOM!

Complete and Unabridged

LINFORD
Leicester

First published in Great Britain

First Linford Edition
published 2005

Copyright © 1946 by John Russell Fearn
Copyright © 2005 by Philip Harbottle

British Library CIP Data

Fearn, John Russell, *1908 – 1960*
 Within that room!.—Large print ed.—
 Linford mystery library
 1. Haunted castles—England—Fiction
 2. Ghost stories 3. Large type books
 I. Title
 823.9'12 [F]

 ISBN 1–84617–035–4

Published by
F. A. Thorpe (Publishing)
Anstey, Leicestershire

Set by Words & Graphics Ltd.
Anstey, Leicestershire
Printed and bound in Great Britain by
T. J. International Ltd., Padstow, Cornwall

This book is printed on acid-free paper

1

There was nothing else for it but to get on the move — to reach London as quickly as possible and there devote what remained of meager savings to a last effort to find suitable employment. Vera Grantham had come to this conclusion slowly, had fought against its inevitability, though she had known all the time that it would finally be forced upon her.

She had emerged from the A.T.S. full of hopes and plans, only to discover that she was one of millions with similar hopes and plans. Her gratuity and savings could not last indefinitely, so —

'Nothing else offers so I'll have to do it!' she decided, sighing, and she pushed away the piece of paper upon which she had been making figures. Whichever way she had added them up they had still shown a total of £25 on the wrong side and a balance of £15 in the bank.

'Which isn't much for a bouncing girl

full of health, hope and ambition,' she muttered.

She tried to smile at her misfortune as she sat at the little table in her small room, but just the same it was worry which impelled her hand through her thick blonde hair; it was worry which had brought little lines of strain round the clear blue eyes and puckers to her firm mouth. Vera Grantham, aged 24, blessed with a courage that had defied shells and bombs, now faced a problem that had so far defeated her.

As she sat thinking, gazing absently through the window on to a huddle of gray, dreary rooftops in the hot June sunshine, there came a light tap on the door.

'Are you there, love?'

It was Mrs. Hallam, Vera's landlady — very generous, very ample, very Lancashire.

'Yes, Mrs. Hallam. Come in.'

Ponderous, gray-haired, enveloped in a large check apron, Mrs. Hallam entered.

'There's a gent downstairs, love,' she said, her manner confidential. ''E says he wants to see you.'

'Oh?' Then Vera's moody expression changed. 'Oh! Does he? What does he look like?'

'Well, 'e's smart like, with a dark suit. 'E's got a flat leather case with 'im. Hoff 'and I'd say 'es a lawyer or somethin'.'

Vera got up and closed the door. Then she came back with a thoughtful frown to the surprised Mrs. Hallam.

'Mrs. Hallam,' she said, 'You've been a very good friend to me, so I think it is only fair that you should know how I stand. I'm — well, about broke. A lot of unpaid bills have mounted up since I was demobbed, and I can't pay them. That little man down below has probably come with a summons. In other words, I've got to get out. I was just thinking it over when you knocked on the door.'

Mrs. Hallam looked at the girl's serious face. 'But, Vera, where'll you go?'

'Where everybody goes when they're down on their luck,' Vera smiled. 'London. Manchester is no good to me, even though I was born and raised here. There don't seem to be any openings for a commercial artist, and nothing else will do for me. So I'll pay what rent I owe and then be on my way. I know a man in London who might be able to help me, if bombs and rockets haven't blasted him out of business.'

'But — what do I do with that there man down below?' Mrs. Hallam asked.

'Well, it depends on what you told him. What did you say about me?' Mrs. Hallam smiled complacently.

'I told 'im I'd see if you was in. 'E said to tell you 'is name is Thwaite, of Morgan, Thwaite and 'Endricks.'

'Then he is a solicitor!' Vera exclaimed, snapping her fingers. 'That means a writ! Tell him I'm out. Get rid of him. I'm going to start packing.'

Mrs. Hallam nodded and left the room. The instant the door was shut, Vera turned quickly and dragged her suitcase from under the bed, began to pack it with her modest belongings and leftovers from the A.T.S. — including a gas mask which she had forgotten to turn in at the depot.

She hummed softly to herself, happy now that she had a plan in mind. The fact

4

that its success was not assured was of no consequence; she was on the move and that was the main thing.

It did not take her more than 10 minutes to complete her packing. She was just putting on her hat and coat when Mrs. Hallam knocked and re-entered.

'I got rid of 'im, love,' she said, beaming. 'Mind yer, I don't think 'e believed what I told 'im, but 'e went just the same and said e'd come back tonight.'

Vera smiled in relief. 'I'll be in London by then, and since I don't know where I'm going to settle you can't give a forwarding address. Now, how much do I owe you?'

'It'll be 12 and six up today, love — but if you're 'ard pressed just leave it. Call it square until you get started fair and proper like — '

'No, no. I must be independent if I can, Mrs. Hallam — it's part of my nature. That's why I feel so awful at having piled up these bills which I can't pay; at least not yet.' Vera rummaged in her handbag. 'There you are — 12 and six, and thanks for being so good to me.'

'It's been a pleasure I'm sure. I only 'opes you do all right among them Londoners. You ought to, with your face and figure.'

'I'm afraid they haven't much selling value to a commercial artist,' Vera sighed — then she looked momentarily surprised as Mrs. Hallam threw her arms about her and gave her a warm kiss.

'Just for luck, love,' she explained, and insisted on seeing the girl down to the street.

As she left the house and waved back, Vera felt as though she were leaving behind a very generous soul. She knew she could never hope to find a kinder landlady than Mrs. Hallam; but in another sense the prospect of change, of fighting for opportunity in London, stirred her young and spirited soul to the challenge.

At the 'bus stop she set down her case beside her and wondered whether she ought to take off her coat in the warm sunshine. She was still trying to make up her mind when she caught sight of two things one after the other. The bus she

6

wanted was speeding toward her, while from out of the street she had just left, a small man in bowler hat was emerging. He was dressed in dark clothes and carrying a briefcase. It did not have to be Mr. Thwaite, of course, but all the same . . .

Vera hastily boarded the 'bus, and found a seat on the lower deck. The legal-looking man also boarded and went upstairs. Vera sat wondering and frowning, so much so that she vaguely resented the presence of the conductor asking for her fare.

At London Road station she took up her case and alighted. Glancing back, she saw that the annoying little man with the briefcase was walking swiftly after her — so she put on speed, mingled with the crowd inside the station, and as far as she could tell managed to lose her pursuer. Unless, of course, there was always the chance he was not Mr. Thwaite at all.

Vera bought her ticket to London and to her relief found the 10.50 already waiting at platform 1. Complimenting herself on her evasive action in face of the enemy she selected a compartment, heaved her case up on the rack, then settled down in a corner seat furthest from the corridor.

When the train had been an hour on its way, however, her complacency was shattered. As she sat reading in her corner she happened to glance up to behold a bowler-hatted figure in dark clothes moving along the corridor. He peered into her compartment, looking straight at her, then at her four travelling companions. Inwardly she began to quiver with indignation, was right on the verge of jumping up and demanding to know what he wanted — then remembering it could only be a summons, she remained still and waited. The little man moved on — but Vera had not the least doubt that he was hovering in the corridor just out of her line of vision.

When she left the compartment in search of the dining car, she glanced casually over her shoulder. Sure enough, there he was. He seemed about to raise a hand at her in signal but she turned away so quickly she could not be sure of it.

When she entered the dining car she whipped up a menu quickly and sat peeping over it.

Presently the little man came drifting in. He was forestalled in his approach, however, by the waiter. Vera gave her order and then sat back and looked icily through the pursuer as he dodged in the background. Quite undeterred, though, he came forward, taking off his bowler hat to reveal a bald head fringed with gray fluff.

'Excuse me, but — are you Miss Vera Grantham?' he asked.

His voice was quiet enough, Vera decided, and quite cultured — but she remained coldly uncompromising.

'I am. And if you don't stop following me, I intend to inform the guard! I strongly object to it!'

2

'You are quite within your rights, Miss Grantham, and I really must apologise. If it were not so important a matter I — '

'It must be!' Vera interrupted. 'You have never stopped chasing me since I left my room in Manchester!'

The little man put his hat down on one of the chairs, and then seated himself beside it.

'Forgive me, Miss Grantham, but this is something which cannot wait — You don't mind my sitting at your table?'

'I don't own the train, do I?'

'Hmmm — no, of course not. Er — Here is my card.' Vera took it though she knew what was coming —

Jonathan Thwaite Morgan,
Thwaite & Hendricks
Solicitors
Brazennose St., Manchester

'Very interesting,' Vera said. 'But it's no surprise . . . '

She looked at him steadily and read puzzlement in his eyes. It was as though he could not understand her distant manner.

'You go to quite a lot of trouble to serve a summons, don't you?' Vera asked.

'Summons?' Jonathan Thwaite looked as though the word were in a foreign language. 'Summons?' he repeated. 'Whatever gave you that idea?'

'I can hardly conceive of any other, being up to my neck in debt and with little prospect of paying off — '

'So that's it!' Thwaite laughed so much the gold in his back teeth became revealed. Then he seemed to remember the sobriety of his calling and became serious again. 'No wonder you resented my following you.'

He leaned forward confidentially, but before he could get started the waiter returned with Vera's lunch.

'I'll take the same,' Thwaite said, surveying it: then as the waiter hurried off, he added: 'I'm here to bring you good news, Miss Grantham, and if it is all the same to you, you can transact the business here instead of returning to Manchester. I can get a train back from Crewe.'

'Good news?' Vera was suspicious. 'But you don't even resemble Santa Claus, Mr. Thwaite.'

He coughed away his inner thoughts and laid his briefcase on the table beside him. Then he leaned forward again and asked a question in a hushed voice.

'Do you remember your Uncle Cyrus? Cyrus Merriforth?'

Vera frowned and tried to remember. It required some effort, too.

'Why, yes, I believe I do,' Vera assented. 'Only vaguely, though. I met him once when I was a girl at school. I seem to remember that he was a world traveller, always hopping about collecting butter-flies and plants or something, then coming home and writing books about them.'

'Your uncle was a very famous ento-mologist and botanist, Miss Grantham.'

'Knew his bugs?' Vera suggested calmly.

'Hum! Ha! Yes, indeed!'

Thwaite paused as his lunch was set before him. He looked at it and then cleared his throat.

'We are his solicitors,' he resumed. 'He learned during the war of your gallantry in the A.T.S. — of which there was some mention in the newspapers — and decided on that account to add a codicil to his will. Now that he is dead we — '

'Oh, he's dead!' Vera said.

'Yes, yes, of course.' Thwaite looked irritable. 'He died a little while ago and was cremated.'

'I'm sorry, Mr. Thwaite, but you hadn't told me he was dead. He added a codicil, a codicil because of me?' Vera wrestled with the unexpected. 'But — but why me?' she asked blankly. 'Didn't he remember my mother, his own sister? Though she died in the blitz along with my father, my uncle did not know that . . . '

'The codicil refers entirely to you,' Thwaite stated, brushing away the side issues.

'And he left me a huge fortune, I

suppose?' Vera shook her blonde head. 'I just don't believe it! Remote uncles only leave fortunes to half forgotten nieces in novels.'

Thwaite coughed and looked at his lunch.

'No, Miss Grantham,' he admitted, 'he did not leave you a fortune.'

Vera sighed, and picked up her knife and fork again. 'I knew it! What then? A butterfly net and an old magnifying glass?'

'He left you Sunny Acres and £100. The bulk of his fortune went to the Society for the Preservation of Ancient Flora and Fauna; that is except for an annuity to his two servants, Mr. and Mrs. Falworth.'

Vera smiled sadly. Then her blue eyes began to take on a new light. 'What do you mean by Sunny Acres?'

'It is the residence which Mr. Merriforth owned. It is far more than a mere residence. It is a one-time feudal castle. It has extensive grounds, and, should you wish to sell, could probably realize £15,000 for it. Such an offer is indeed

14

already in existence. Do you know Surrey at all? The little hamlet of Waylock Dean?'

'Fifteen thou — Waylock Dean?' Vera shook her head absently. 'Fifteen thousand! Great Scot!'

'The residence,' Thwaite proceeded, 'has the two servants already installed — Mr. and Mrs. Falworth. They are a middle-aged couple, the woman being housekeeper, cook and so forth; while the man does the gardening and odd jobs. They've been at Sunny Acres for the past 10 years.'

'And the old boy left it all to me?' Vera asked incredulously. 'All because of some trifling act I performed which was considered brave enough to merit mention in the newspapers! Good heavens! I always knew the old chap was a bit eccentric and now I'm sure of it. Incidentally, what is the £100 for?'

'I have not the least idea, Miss Grantham — unless it is intended as incidental expenses. The moment your uncle died and his will had been proved, it became our duty, of course, to trace you. We managed it through the ministry of labour, who had a record of you seeking employment as a commercial artist. I reached your rooming house this morning and was turned away. I felt somehow that things were not quite as they should be, so I decided to wait.'

'And I'm thankful that you did,' Vera declared. 'To think that I might have turned my back on Sunny Acres and £100 if you hadn't been so persistent! I'm sorry if I seemed rude.'

'Considering the circumstances I can quite understand your attitude,' Thwaite said gallantly. Then for a while they continued their lunches as they thought things out. It was Thwaite who finally broke the silence.

'I feel that I should mention one condition,' he said, and Vera gave him a sharp look.

'Condition? So there are strings to it after all.'

'Hardly that, Miss Grantham: it is just a matter of a legend. I have mentioned that Sunny Acres was once a feudal castle. Well, it is considered to be haunted, so much so that no resident of

Waylock Dean will go near the place. Your uncle, I believe, had quite a distressing experience with the phantom about a year ago, and the servants swear that haunting does take place.'

'Old-fashioned bogey stories don't frighten me,' Vera replied. 'Thanks for telling me, though.'

'Am I to understand, then, that you will take Sunny Acres and the hundred pounds?'

'I most certainly will! I had decided this morning to try my luck at getting a job in London — but now I have really got something to travel to! What do I have to do?'

Thwaite opened his briefcase with meticulous care and drew forth a number of legal papers.

'I have everything here, Miss Grantham, to make the business legal. All you have to do is sign. Later on the deed will be forwarded to you . . . '

'I see. And — er — don't think I'm grasping, Mr. Thwaite, but what about that hundred pounds? I'm extremely short of cash at the moment.'

Thwaite smiled, drew forth a sealed envelope, handed it over. Vera opened it and peered inside at 50 one-pound notes and five £10 ones. Then she took her right arm between her left finger and thumb and pinched hard.

'Mmm — must be true! I'm still here!'

'If you will sign here . . . ' Thwaite traced a finger along the bottom of one of the papers and then proffered his fountain pen.

Vera signed, and the scant scattering of diners looked on in polite interest.

She signed the documents that Thwaite replaced in his case. Then he sat back with the air of a man who has done a ticklish job well.

'And you think you will reside at Sunny Acres, Miss Grantham?' he asked.

Vera ate in silence for a while.

'Off-hand, I can't say. I don't really see what use an old feudal castle and a couple of servants will be to me. I'm only 24, unattached, and anxious to make my mark in the artistic world. I'll probably sell the place after spending a few days in it as a sort of holiday. I'd sooner have

£15,000 than a pile of old brick and a ghost. Anyway, I'll see.'

'Until you make up your mind I will address the mail to Sunny Acres,' Thwaite decided. 'Mr. and Mrs. Falworth will be informed by telegram of your coming. I'll send it from Crewe.'

'By telegram? Don't tell me the moated castle hasn't even got a telephone?'

'I'm afraid it hasn't. Your uncle had a decided dislike for modern amenities.'

'I think,' Vera decided, 'that my uncle was a queer old duck whichever way you look at it!'

3

Still feeling very much as though she had walked out of fairyland, and certainly feeling very travel stained and weary, Vera found herself alighting at the wayside station of Waylock Dean about 8 o'clock in the evening. Fortunately the weather was still good. It was warm and windless with a soft June sky from which the daylight was commencing to fade.

Lugging her travelling case, Vera asked the stationmaster, 'Any chance of a conveyance of some sort?'

''Fraid not, miss. Joe knocks off at 7.'

'You don't mean to tell me there's only one conveyance?'

'Just the 'ack, miss, that's all. This ain't a big place.'

'You're telling me. But surely there's something? I'm tired. I've come all the way from Manchester today.'

The man considered. 'It depends, sort of, on 'ow far you be wantin' to go.'

20

'To Sunny Acres, wherever that is.'

The man stared at her fixedly. 'Sunny Acres? You're goin' there? You won't get nobody to take you, miss. An' I'm sorry for you.'

'Well, that's nice of you — and confoundedly helpful too, when my feet are too tired to carry me.'

'Nobody'll go within a mile of Sunny Acres, miss. It's got a ghost, it 'as!'

'Oh, nuts!' Vera said crossly, blowing a stray hair out of her eye. 'I'd pay treble price to be taken there.'

'Sorry. But what a trim young woman like you wants in that hawful place I can't think.'

Shaking his head over mournful thoughts, he turned away. Vera looked after him angrily, and then went outside and along a flower-bordered path to the main street. It ran through the center of a disordered array of small houses and cottages mixed up with shops and a post-office. A small steeple marked the church; a white globe inscribed 'Saddler's Arms' proclaimed the pub; and beyond there was nothing but a backdrop of meadows already melting into the soft mists of evening.

Vera sniffed, and put down her bag while she weighed things up. Presently the stationmaster approached her.

'Thinkin' better of it?' he asked affably. 'There be a train back to London at 9.30. You'd best take it.'

'I'm going to Sunny Acres if it kills me!' Vera retorted. 'Where is the confounded place, anyway? At least tell me that!'

'There!' He pointed and she found herself looking beyond the village to a ring of trees perhaps two miles away. The mists made the view uncertain.

'I don't see any house,' she said.

'The 'ouse be behind them trees, miss. But it ain't an 'ouse; it be a castle, an' it's 'idden away from the decent light o' day.'

Vera picked up her bag and began to walk along Waylock Dean's main street. Just at this moment her thoughts toward the departed Uncle Cyrus were not of the sweetest. She had been tramping with increasing weariness for 10 minutes and had left the village behind when the honking of an ancient motor horn made her glance round. A small car was close behind her.

She moved to one side of the road, but to her surprise the car stopped a little way in front of her. When she caught up with it a sunburned young man in shirt sleeves, his riotous dark hair tumbling round his forehead, was looking out through the driving seat window.

'Want a lift?' he asked.

Vera measured him coldly, but she stopped all the same. Her eyes went over the incredibly ancient car.

'Do I look like that sort of a girl?' Vera asked.

'Frankly, you don't look like anything at all at the moment! Your face is dirty, your hair's straggling, your shoes and stockings are covered in dust — '

Vera elevated her nose, picked up her bag and began to limp on. She had hardly covered five yards before the young man had caught up to her. He was pretty tall, she noticed, and had merry blue eyes, which, with his dark hair, gave him a vaguely Irish appearance.

'Sorry,' he apologised. 'I shouldn't have said that. But you do look all in. If you're willing to trust a young man with quite honest intentions I can help you on your way. I'm going through to Little Twiddleford, if the darn car will hold out. The name is Dick Wilmott, formerly of the R.A.F. At the moment I'm getting together a radio sales and repair connection.'

'In this one-eyed hole?'

'No. I have a small shop over in Godalming — but I give Bertha an airing most evenings to keep her battery charged. That's Bertha,' he added, nodding to the car. 'She's lost her beauty and streamlining, I'm afraid, but you're welcome to ride in her.'

'Well, I like your line better than the awful stuff I was handed by the stationmaster here. I'm Vera Grantham — of Manchester.'

They shook hands frankly, then they both smiled at each other.

'Sir Galahad offers a new type of charger,' Dick Wilmott said, bowing low.

'Which reminds me I need a battery charger, too. Anyway, let me help you madam.'

He took her bag and put it in the back of the car. The upholstering was bursting out, Vera noticed, and there were spare radio parts cluttering up the floor.

'Hmmm — four-seater!' she remarked dryly.

'Two and room for junk,' he corrected. 'Allow me . . . '

He held the front side door open for her, gingerly, as though afraid it might drop off, and she sank down thankfully in the worn seat. On another moment he had scrambled in beside her and stretched long legs towards the clutch and accelerator pedals.

'Where to?' he inquired.

'That place up behind the trees there — Sunny Acres. And if you say 'Poor girl', or something like that I shan't blame you.'

'Why should I?' He started the noisy engine.

'Only that I'm apparently going with my life in my hands in visiting Sunny

Acres. The place is supposed to be haunted.'

'Is it? I wouldn't know. As I told you, I belong to Godalming. One thing I will say, though — you look too nice a girl to be in a backwoods dump like this. Or maybe you've got relations at Sunny Acres?'

'No. I've just taken over the ownership.'

The car wobbled as Dick Wilmott nearly lost his grip on the steering wheel.

'You own it?'

'It was left to me,' Vera explained things briefly.

'So that's how it is? Well, jolly good luck to you. I'd be inclined to sell and get rid of the place. Go and live somewhere cheerful instead of trying to exist in a hole like this. Still, that's for you to decide. Hello, this looks like a road to the castle.'

He branched off on to a narrow side-road leading between hawthorn hedges, and up to massive wrought iron gates. On the stone pillars supporting them the words 'Sunny Acres' had been chiselled — long ago. By this time weather had nearly eroded them.

Dick hopped out and opened the gates, then drove up the drive with its overhanging beech and elm trees to the portico outside the front door. To Vera, studying the place, there was an oppressive aspect about it. It was huge, thickly cloaked in ivy, and the battlements were obviously those of a castle. Even the rounded watch towers with their slits of windows were there. The remainder of the windows seemed to be diamond-shaped and mullioned, some of them being stained glass.

'Not far from the Middle Ages,' Dick commented; then he stopped the car's noisy engine and climbed out to hammer on the massive front door with a griffin knocker. For some reason the reverberation sounded as if he had thumped the lid of a coffin.

Slowly Vera alighted, trying to make up her mind whether she liked the place or not. She tried to convince herself that it was the dying evening light that made everything so depressing, or maybe it was the overgrown trees, or perhaps her fatigue. But deep in her heart she knew it was none of these things. It was an elusive quality which she could only associate with — dread. Sunny Acres, despite its name, somehow crawled with a vague portent of evil.

Abruptly the door was opened and a woman gowned completely in black stood looking out. She was uncommonly tall for a woman, very white skinned, with her dark, shining hair drawn into a trim bun at the back of her head. In a striking kind of way she was handsome, a strongly hooked nose creating a masculine aspect. Her features were impassive.

'Well?' she inquired, in a mellow if uncompromising voice.

'I'm Vera Grantham.'

This seemed to animate the woman at once.

'Oh, Miss Grantham — of course! I am sorry.'

'This is Mr Wilmott,' Vera said. 'He was good enough to give me a lift.'

'I see. Come in, won't you? I'll have my husband carry in your bag.'

'I'll do it,' Dick volunteered, and going back to the car he lifted out the suitcase and then followed Vera and the woman into the hall.

The hall was broad, square, and gloomy. There were two mullioned windows that permitted faded light to drift through the glint indifferently upon armory, and innumerable brass plaques. In the sombre distances a huge staircase loomed. The floor was apparently composed of granite, roughened on the surface, and practically covered with costly rugs and mats lying at various angles.

Instinctively Vera crossed her arms and gripped opposite shoulders. She gave a troubled little smile.

'Cold, isn't it?' she said.

'Central heating is not installed, Miss Grantham,' Mrs. Falworth explained calmly. 'Naturally a residence of this size does become chilly, even in summer, especially so late in the evening.'

'Well, having got you this far,' Dick Wilmott said, 'I think I'll be off. Glad to have been able to help you.'

Vera looked at him with unintentional longing.

'You really have to go? You couldn't stay and have a little refreshment?'

'I'm afraid not. Thanks all the same. I simply must hop over to Little Twiddleford, and then I've got to get back to Godalming. I don't want to leave it too late in case that battery of mine dies on me when I light up. Glad to have met you.' He hesitated, and said: 'You can always reach me at my shop in Gordon St., Godalming, or you can ring Godalming 72.'

He took Vera's slender hand in a broad palm and squeezed her fingers generously. Then, whistling to himself, he swung out through the front doorway and went down to his car. Vera stood listening with a sinking heart to the fading noise of his old wreck. When he had gone, Mrs. Falworth closed the front door and pushed across the heavy bolts.

'I do not think there will be any more callers tonight, Miss,' she said gravely, hovering black-gowned and impersonal in the now intensified shadows.

'No, I suppose not,' Vera said, making an effort to get a grip on herself. 'I'd like to freshen up. I've been doing a good deal of travelling.'

'I am sure you have, miss. If you will come this way? I will have my husband bring up your bag afterward.'

Vera followed the tall figure across the hall and up the broad staircase. The steps were of polished stone with a carpet running down the center. Everything was massive. There were great stone pillars supporting the cupola that formed the hall ceiling; the doors of the lower rooms leading off the hall were all beaten oak and fitted with heavy copper hinges. And everything was so dreadfully cold that Vera hugged herself again.

They went along a wide corridor with doors leading off either side of it. A huge stained-glass window provided illumination. Being at a higher elevation the sun was casting its last rays through in an uncertain spectrum.

'This, Miss Grantham, is the east wing,' Mrs. Falworth said. 'The west wing is not used.'

Vera said nothing. She felt rather like a new girl in a college as she followed the housekeeper to the third doorway on the left. It was opened for her and she stepped into a huge bedroom. It took her breath away for the moment. There was a vast fireplace and two windows of mullion pattern with ivy fringing their edges. There were rugs on the stone floor. The furniture was old, with a four-poster bed.

4

'This — is my room?' Vera asked, turning.

Mrs. Falworth inclined her dark head gravely.

'Yes, miss. I trust it meets with your approval?'

'Oh, yes — yes surely. Only it's a bit — stuffy.'

'Stuffy, miss?'

'Well, old-fashioned. I prefer modern things. I'm a modern girl, you know, and I've learned to appreciate streamlining.'

Not a trace of expression showed on the housekeeper's Red Indian features, but she did condescend to gesture slightly.

'I am afraid that your uncle was not abreast of the times. He preferred antiques to modernity. Whatever changes you may wish to make I shall be happy to discuss with you later. Dinner will be served in the dining-hall at 9 o'clock. Usually, it is at 7.'

Vera nodded slowly. 'Thanks. Oh, where is there a bathroom in this wilderness?'

'There are three in this wing — down the corridor which branches to the left. They are all contained in what used to be an outlook tower. However, that door over there,' the housekeeper said indicating one in a corner of the bedroom, 'opens into your private bathroom and dressing-room. I think you will find everything in order.'

Mrs. Falworth seemed to think that she had done all that was needful for she gave a slight inclination of the head and went out. Vera stood looking about her for a moment, then she pulled off her hat and coat and tossed them on the bed. Pondering, she began to walk round — until she caught sight of her dishevelled appearance in the mirror.

'Good heavens, Vera, is that you?' she asked her reflection.

Sitting down at the dressing table she picked up the brush and comb and began her activities, pausing presently as there came a knock at the door. In response to her invitation to come in an elderly man entered — square-shouldered, gray-haired, with a crinkled face. He conveyed with him an air of heavy trouble — a definitely henpecked look. Carefully he set down Vera's suitcase at the foot of the bed.

'You'll be Mr. Falworth?' Vera asked him, smiling.

'That's right, miss, I am. Happy I am to welcome you, too, only — only I'd be much happier if you were leaving instead.'

'I suppose,' Vera said slowly, 'you are not related to the old man down at the station? The one who takes the tickets?'

'Sam Hitchin? No, I'm not related, miss.'

'I just wondered because he said the same thing as you've just said — that I'd be better off going than coming. Some nonsense about this place being haunted.'

Old man Falworth looked troubled.

'That's just it, miss. It isn't nonsense — it's horribly true. A ghost does exist and there is an evil presence throughout this whole house. It isn't my place to say too much, and I know my wife won't because she believes in the supernatural.

I'm just a plain, honest man, miss, and I'm telling you — do not stay here.'

Vera hesitated, a question in the back of her mind. Then she shrugged it away, and picked up the brush and comb again.

'Ghosts don't worry me. And thanks for bringing my bag.'

'If you want me just pull one of the bell cords,' Falworth said, and went shuffling out.

Vera, from that moment, began turning things over in her mind. She meditated while she tied up her yellow tresses into a tight knob; she still meditated while she bathed in tepid water in the bathroom adjoining — and by the time she had changed her attire and restored her hair to its normal waves and curls her thoughts had ended in a blank wall.

Definitely, though, her interest was aroused. The bunkum of ghosts she did not credit for a moment — yet she could not rid herself of the sense of brooding horror the castle possessed. Her common sense told her that a phantom must have a logical explanation which she ought to discover; but her inner fears at being forced to solve the problem alone led her to ponder the advantages of selling the whole antique pile and netting a small fortune in consequence.

She was in a pensive mood as she made her way downstairs and, after some difficulty, found her way to the dining room. Like everything else it was huge — literally a baronial hall with the usual Gothic type of ceiling, two fireplaces — both empty — an enormous sideboard and an immense table laid for one.

Feeling very small and remote she sat down and waited for the impassive Mrs. Falworth to go into action. And Mrs. Falworth did, first placing a bowl of steaming soup on the table.

'Bit dark in here, isn't it?' Vera murmured, tasting the soup and finding it excellent.

'I will light the lamps if you wish, miss.'

'Lamps? Great Scot!' Vera looked above her, and then about her. Over her head hung a wrought iron chandelier with three oil lamps. On the walls were similar lamps fitted into universal sockets.

'Usually I do not light them until the

last spark of daylight has gone,' Mrs. Falworth explained. 'Your uncle believed — as I do — that it is the twilight when this world and the next are almost in contact!'

Vera swallowed some soup so hastily that she burned her tongue. It snapped her out of her attitude of calm wonder.

'Mrs Falworth,' she said, 'I've no intention of sitting here in the dark for spooks or anything else! Turn the lamps on! I — I mean light them. And why on earth isn't there some electricity in the place?'

'Your uncle, miss, did not — '

'I know, he didn't approve! I was always told that he was a trifle eccentric; now I'm sure that he was plain crazy! Don't you realise that this is a modern age? Or didn't you ever hear of the war that was just fought?'

'Our communication with the outside world has certainly not been very extensive,' the housekeeper admitted. 'We have no radio, no telephone, no car, no electric light — '

'And no hot water,' said Vera. 'If it

hadn't have been a summer evening I'd have frozen to death when I bathed just now.'

'I am sorry, miss. The water heater in the kitchen is not as efficient as it might be — You are enjoying your soup?'

'Yes,' Vera admitted. 'You're a first-class cook.'

'I am so glad there is something which pleases you, miss.'

With this doubtful observation, Mrs. Falworth struck a match, and then lighted a long, waxed stick. Holding it like a torch, she went around the array of lamps and lighted them. An uncertain yellow glimmer set the shadows flickering as the daylight fled. But Vera was not too scared to enjoy her meal. Nor was there any fault to find with it. From beginning to end it was a masterpiece of cookery art.

'Now,' Vera said, when it was over, 'I want a word with you, Mrs. Falworth . . .' She sat back in the hard chair and lit a cigarette. 'I want to know why people shy away when this place is mentioned. What is the matter with it?'

'An evil power has had possession of it

for a long time, miss. Such things no human can prevent.'

'You mean a poltergeist?'

'You might call it such miss, even though the exact definition of that term means a violent phantom — a smasher of furniture, and so forth.'

'Oh, then this one does not smash up the happy home, then?'

'Not altogether, no,' Mrs. Falworth stood quite still and hands clasped in front of her. 'The phantom — the manifestation — is seen once a year, but the spirit of evil is here all the time.'

'Well,' Vera said, 'I don't notice it — not particularly, anyway.'

'Not here, perhaps. It has its core in one of the upper rooms, but the influence it spreads can be detected anywhere. You will sense it — in time.'

'You and your husband have been here some years, and yet you haven't gone crazy? Or have you?' Vera added under her breath.

'For me, miss, the psychic world holds no terrors. I understand it fully. I know how to defy the power of evil and darkness — but I cannot say the same for my husband. He is worldly, so essentially mortal, and he is frightened.'

'Then why on earth does he stay here? He's got a mind of his own, hasn't he?'

'I have persuaded him. I feel — and I have brought him round to my way of thinking — that it is our duty to remain as servants to you, as we were servants to your uncle for 10 years.'

'And what if I decided to sell the place?'

For a moment a gleam came into Mrs. Falworth's dark eyes.

'In that event we could leave, miss, with no sense of worry on our minds. If you would sell, it would relieve all three of us. I believe in all seriousness, that this place is not fit for anybody to live in, especially an attractive young woman like you.'

'Why, does the ghost like blonde females?' Vera asked dryly.

'I did not mean it in that sense — rather, I meant that you have too many charms to waste them in a place like this. It is too gloomy and cheerless for a modern young lady.'

Vera said: 'I don't expect to be here all the time. I am seeking a post in London as a commercial artist.'

'Forgive me mentioning it, miss, but do you think such a post would provide sufficient remuneration to keep this residence going?'

'Oh, it might. I presume the upkeep isn't terrific, and as I saw from the conveyance Mr. Thwaite had me sign this land is freehold, so there is no ground rent. No electricity to pay for, and paraffin isn't dear. There is only food to consider and the salaries of you and your husband. Yes, I might be able to keep it going for a while, anyway. In fact, I might even grow to like it. I'll be quite frank, I don't believe in this ghost rubbish.'

'I have spoken the truth, miss,' Mrs. Falworth answered coldly.

'All right — you have your views and I have mine.' Vera got to her feet decisively. 'Now, how about a tour round the place? I want to see what I have inherited. And, by the way, what is your salary, and your husbands?'

'That matter hardly need concern you,

madam. Your uncle, by his will, left both of us amply provided for — '

'Of course! The annuity.'

'Since we must live somewhere, we are prepared to stay here and give service in return for shelter.'

'Oh?' Vera raised her brows in surprise. 'Well, that's very sporting of both of you. Make it all the easier for me to run the show.'

But inwardly she felt that there was something queer, somewhere, though at that moment she could not decide for the life of her what it was . . . She spoke little thereafter as Mrs. Falworth, with a spluttering torch in hand, took her on a tour of inspection.

5

They went through the oil-lighted regions. Then they explored the rambling conservatories and broken-down stables which, after a bit of restoration, might hold a car. From here they descended into a dingy abyss of basements. The cold down here was a shock to Vera and she stood looking round on stony emptiness. There were gray walls with rings in them; a ceiling of granite with rusty hooks imbedded in the stone.

'What are the rings for?' Vera questioned.

'I believe, miss, that this was once a torture chamber. The prisoners were fastened to those rings in the wall, their arms outspread, and then they were 'persuaded' with the help of the old forge there.'

The woman nodded to a corner where stood an ancient fireplace — similar to the type used by a blacksmith. The back had collapsed inward amidst a mass of bricks and oddly coloured red-brown ash. At the back of it was a black square denoting the flue. Projecting from the side was the curved handle that had once worked the bellows.

'You will observe the branding irons,' the housekeeper said, indicating an array of differently shaped bars in a rack above the fireplace. 'Irons for every type of persuasion. For burning of the skin, for obliteration of the eyes, for — '

'All right, all right,' Vera interrupted. 'You needn't bother. What are the hooks for?'

She looked above her and the ghost of a sadistic smile crossed Mrs. Falworth's face.

'For hanging purposes purely, Miss. I have little doubt that victims were suspended up there in all manner of positions in the old days. Medieval, of course, but I am sure it must have been most effective.'

'Must have been,' Vera agreed. She looked around quickly for something to change the subject — and found it. 'Is that another cellar there?' she asked. 'That door?'

'That is an ancient wine cellar, miss — empty of wine, I regret to say. We use it now for the storage of disused articles.'

Vera's blue eyes moved again around the chasing shadows. The gloom, the silence, the spitting of the waxed torch: they were horrible things. Medieval, slinking unbidden into her soul. 'Let's get back upstairs!' she said abruptly.

So they left the basement by the stone steps that led out at the side of the main staircase in the hall. From here the tour continued, covering Uncle Cyrus' library — remarkable for its many showcases containing dried plants and insects — the huge drawing-room; then up the stairs to each of the 12 bedrooms. Of them all, fully furnished, only two were in use — Vera's own, and the Falworths', two rooms removed from her. But there was yet one other room at the far end of the corridor, the edges of the door taped, and heavy screws driven through the door into the frame.

'What's in here?' Vera asked curiously,

46

stopping beside it.

'That, miss, is *the* room,' the house-keeper answered, holding the torch high over their heads.

'Where the ghost walks, you mean?'

'Within that room is a core of evil manifestation — and I would warn you never to enter it if you value your life and reason.'

Vera's firm little chin began to set. She turned and looked at the housekeeper coldly.

'Look here, Mrs. Falworth, do you suggest that I own this house and yet have one room in it forever locked — always wondering what is inside it? I'm not that kind of a girl. It has got to be opened tomorrow. I intend to put an end to this phantom nonsense once and for all.'

The housekeeper stood erect, forbidding. 'I do not wish to seem disrespectful, miss, but I must refuse to obey that order. I will not under any circumstances open that door!'

'Then your husband must.'

'I am sorry, but I shall not permit him to.'

A glint came in Vera's eyes. She said: 'Maybe you have forgotten that it is I who give the orders here? You won't permit him, indeed! If I say this door is to be opened, it will be opened!'

Mrs. Falworth relaxed her frozen attitude suddenly. She caught hold of Vera's arm.

'Miss Grantham, won't you please see that I am trying to save you from an unimaginable disaster? I tell you — I swear to you — that if you go in that room your senses, your reason, will be blasted right out of you!'

Vera stared at her.

'But how do you know that such a horrible thing will happen?'

'Because it has happened before! Your uncle went into this room last year to lay the ghost, and he emerged just on the borderline of insanity! For many months he was raving and it took every bit of my nursing skill and Dr. Gillingham's medical knowledge — he is the village practitioner — to restore his health.

'Even then, we were not very successful for his dreadful experience undoubtedly hastened his end. This room does not contain just a commonplace spirit or apparition; in fact the ghost is only visible once a year, but an overwhelming sense of evil even though the room is empty. That evil can destroy you, mentally and bodily!'

'Well!' Vera looked at the door and then folded her arms. 'To think of that! A piece of screwed up wood between me and the booby hatch! Who fastened the door like this anyway?'

'It was done at your uncle's order last year, after he had entered here. He had the key thrown away and the room has never been entered since.'

Vera considered for a while, then she gave a shrug.

'Well, for the moment I'll leave the matter alone, but I intend to have this room opened finally, so you may as well make up your mind to it. At the moment I am rather too sleepy to care about anything, ghosts included. Does this end the tour?'

'Unless you wish to see the closed wing?'

'Not tonight.'

'Then you have seen everything, miss.'

'Not quite everything, Mrs. Falworth,' Vera said. 'Anyway, thank you for showing me round. I'll go on to bed, I think, while I am upstairs.'

The housekeeper nodded. She was her tall, impassive self again with that strange light shining in her dark eyes.

★   ★   ★

To Vera, despite her trying day with its unexpected excitements, there came little desire for sleep. She was overtired and could not compose herself as she lay awake in the big old-fashioned bedroom thinking over all she had seen and done. Once or twice she must have dozed, but only briefly. Then toward 3 in the morning, according to the big grandfather clock in the hall, which seemed to chime with needless somberness, she heard a sound in the corridor — the softest of footsteps.

For a time she lay listening intently, half expecting to see the knob on her locked door move back and forth in the moonlight. But nothing happened and the sound presently died away. The huge residence was deathly still again.

The only explanation for the sound seemed to be that the Falworths were on the prowl. Vera got out of bed and into her dressing gown and slippers. Picking up the old poker from the fireplace she tiptoed to the door and unlocked it. Opening it an inch she listened. There was no sound save the tick-tock of the grandfather clock below.

'Well, come what may, here I go,' she said to herself, and went into the corridor.

It was deserted — with the moon casting a faint tracery of coloured beams through the stained glass window. Feeling none too sure of herself, Vera crept to the staircase and then went down it silently, pausing to listen at every five steps.

She had gained the bottom when the first sounds reached her — curious sounds, like the clanking of two pieces of metal on each other.

She frowned in bewilderment and looked over the staircase's stone rail at the dim, shadowy outline of the door leading into the basement. It was from that spot that the sounds had come. She took a firmer grip of the poker and went to the cellar door and opened it. Down below everything was dark but there were sounds, the unmistakable clink of metal and an odd swishing sound as though somebody were having a bath.

For quite a while Vera hesitated, then clinging to the basement stair-rail with her free hand she felt her way down into the darkness. But she only got halfway down before her nerve began to fail her. Alone here in this strange old house, facing a doubtful old man and an icily respectful house-keeper — It was no place to be at 3 in the morning.

Then there came to her an awful smell. It surged up in waves as she went lower. It seemed to be drifting from the direction of a thin bar of light low down in the gloom. Holding her nose and staring fixedly, Vera saw that it was leaking from under the door of the cellar Mrs.

Falworth had said was full of disused articles.

Vera realised it required no genius to judge that all was not as it should be in Sunny Acres. Quite the opposite, in fact. Finally, though, curiosity overrode fears and she crept down the remaining steps. When she reached the door she looked at the bar of light showing below it and then listened to the clanking and swishing sounds beyond it.

Finally she lay flat and put her eye to the narrow crack. In the wavering glow of an oil lamp she could see something metallic and the feet of a man and a woman — presumably the Falworths — as they moved about. Nothing more.

Worried, Vera stood up again, debating. Then as there came the sound of a latch moving on the door's other side she whisked up the flowing skirt of her gown and fled for the steps, blundering up them as best she could in the dark and emerging breathlessly in the hall. As fast as possible she got back in her bedroom and locked the door, her brain whirling.

'A phantom, people who work in the

cellar at dead of night, a smell like the drains gone wrong! What sort of place did Uncle Cyrus wish on to me, anyhow?'

Since she could not answer her own question she forced herself to give up thinking about the matter and instead went to bed to try to catch up on some much needed sleep. And she succeeded — for it was dawn when she awoke and one thought was clear in her mind as she opened her eyes lazily.

She had got to have help — and quickly.

6

Dick Wilmott was busy in his little radio shop in Godalming next morning when Vera walked in.

He turned from the bench where he was working, preparing his best smile for approaching business — then his eyebrows rose.

'Well, blow me down — the girl from Manchester!' he exclaimed. 'This is a surprise and a grand one. Er — there's a chair here somewhere.'

Vera laughed as he looked anxiously round amidst a little of radio equipment, packing cases, shavings, and various odds and ends.

'Never mind,' she said, 'I'm not a physical wreck just yet, though I have suspicions that I soon shall be if I don't watch out.'

Dick pushed back his tumbled dark hair. 'Sorry — about the chair. You know how it is when you're setting up in business: everything gets cockeyed. Anyway, I'm darned glad to see you. He smiled faintly.

'Feel like indulging in a radio set? Cost price to you, you know — '

'My housekeeper believes that I have come out for that very purpose,' Vera answered seriously. 'But I haven't. It's something else.'

'Oh?' Dick tried not to show disappointment. 'What then?'

'I don't quite know how you're going to take this, Mr. Wilmott . . . ' Vera traced a meaningless design with her finger on the packing case beside her. 'I'm in need of help. There is something very queer about Sunny Acres.'

'What's wrong with it? And do sit down,' Dick urged, dusting the top of a packing case vigorously with a sheet of soft paper. 'I hate to see a girl standing. There! That's better!'

Vera settled daintily on the case's edge and put down her handbag beside her.

'Mr. Wilmott,' she said, her serious blue eyes fixing on him. 'I'm facing a legend, a phantom, an aura of evil, and — I think — counterfeiters.'

Dick half smiled. 'Quite a load for a girl on her own! Sure you haven't missed anything out?'

'Matter of fact, yes. There's the odd matter of an abominable smell.'

'Probably the old age of the place!'

'You don't believe me, do you?' Vera asked quietly.

'Oh, I don't say that exactly, but perhaps you've imagined part of it. For one thing, phantoms do not exist, and as for counterfeiters they are more in the line of hoary melodrama than a country residence.'

He held out his cigarette case and then flicked his lighter into flame. Over the haze of smoke they considered each other — and both liked what they saw.

'Mr. Wilmott, would you call a room with a sealed and nailed door pure imagination? Would you call it imagination when my housekeeper swears that to enter that room will cause me to either die or lose my reason?'

Dick Wilmott's expression changed

slightly. 'And the counterfeiters and the smell?'

Vera outlined every incident as it had occurred. His levity had entirely gone when she had finished.

'You're not lacking in nerve, are you?' Dick asked.

'No,' Vera answered. 'I got that way in the A.T.S. — but I feel sort of alone and hemmed in. I don't know a soul in the district except you. I can't talk to Mrs. Falworth and her husband, and so — Well, it's mighty queer. Besides, the Falworths — Mrs. Falworth anyway — don't want wages. They had an annuity left them by my uncle. Did you ever hear of two people being willing to go on working, and in a haunted castle at that, just so that they can give service and have a roof over their heads? I'm quite sure housing shortage isn't the answer . . . Taking it all round, Mr. Wilmott, what do you think is going on?'

'Off-hand, I'd say something fishy. That castle is no place where I'd like my sister to live, or my wife — if I had either. Why don't you sell the place?'

'I have thought about it. According to my lawyer there is a prospective buyer who would pay £15,000 for it.'

'Then sell! Get out! Retire and live in comfort. I would.'

'Would you?' Vera asked. 'Knowing things are not as they should be? Even knowing you have been too scared to probe into the mystery of a so-called evil presence?'

Dick dropped his cigarette on the floor and ground it under his heel. He gave a rueful grin, then said:

'You don't want to feel that you ran out like a coward? You'd rather discover what's going on?'

'Much rather,' Vera acknowledged. 'And I wondered if you would help me?'

There was silence in the little store for a moment. Dick Wilmott stood with his thumbs hooked on his belt, staring at the floor. From his pursed-up lips Vera judged that quite a few thoughts were passing through his mind.

'Naturally,' she added, 'it would be quite ethical. Mr. and Mrs. Falworth are in themselves chaperones. But you see I felt that if I could have somebody with me who is no more afraid of supernatural bunk than I am — and a man too — we could do such a lot. Even sort the whole thing out. After all, if there is something criminal going on it is up to us as public-spirited citizens to stop it, isn't it?'

'What about getting the police?' Dick asked.

'Show me the police who believe in ghosts! And as for the counterfeiting — well, if I should be wrong, think of the mess I'd get myself into!'

Dick began to smile slowly. 'You know,' he said, cocking a merry blue eye upon her, 'you're not fooling me a bit!'

'Meaning?' Vera asked coldly.

'That you're like all the rest of your sex — barring the man-eating, flat-shoed variety. You're enough of a woman to want a man to help you when things get alarming. Slang us all you like when things are okay, but at the least hint of the mysterious — Wow!'

'You flatter yourself, Mr. Wilmott,' Vera kept her face perfectly straight. 'It is simply that you are the only person I can turn to in this dilemma, and so — '

'Well, I'll see what I can do. And if it comes to that, why not? I didn't get half enough time last night to get acquainted anyway. Incidentally, why don't you call me Dick?'

'All right then, Dick — what are you going to do?'

'Go back with you and try to sort the thing out — '

'But what about your business? That's what worries me!'

'I can't open in real earnest until I get my trade license from the government. Until then I'm limited to repairs and one or two pre-war radios. And anyway, what sort of a chap do you think I am? Pass up the chance to help a blonde in distress? Not likely! I told you last night that there is a lot of Sir Galahad in me. But,' Dick finished, 'there is something bothering me. How do you propose to explain me to that fire-eater of a housekeeper? It's going to look a bit odd — you coming to buy a radio and returning with me instead! You told her last night that I had merely given you a lift.'

Vera hesitated and wished that she could control the gentle wave of color she could feel stealing over her cheeks.

'I wondered if we might not pretend to — to be engaged? That would take care of a lot of proprieties. I would explain away your visit last night — somehow.'

Dick's eyebrows went up. 'Gosh, you have thought of everything, haven't you? But why should we just pretend to be engaged?'

'Oh, really now, Mr. Wil — I mean, Dick! This is a sort of business arrangement — '

'Well, never mind. If you want a game of 'let's pretend' I'm willing. How about the ring?'

Vera pulled a small jewelled ring from a finger of her right hand and transferred it to the third on her left.

'That'll do,' she said, trying to appear unconcerned. 'Now to all intents and purposes, we are engaged.'

'Right! Vera, you have made yourself my wife to be!'

She looked at him rather blankly. His

free use of her Christian name had sounded quite odd, but all the same — Mmmm . . . it had not sounded so bad, either.

In a few minutes he accompanied her outside and locked the door.

'I don't think Bertha is quite the right vehicle for a bride-to-be,' he decided. 'All right for that lift last night, but that's about all. I think we'd better take a 'bus. Come on.'

Vera nodded. She did not quite like the indulgent way he kept smiling at her, as though she were a child who had done something silly and had been obliged to confess to the fact.

As they walked along the street, he asked, 'Is there anything we should know about each other before we meet the dragon?'

'Nothing at all. Mrs. Falworth doesn't know a thing about me, except I am the niece of the late Cyrus Merriforth; and of course she doesn't know anything about you, either.'

'I shall be obliged, of course, to call you 'dearest' and 'darling' quite a lot,' Dick reflected. 'You have realized that, I suppose?'

'Yes, but take care you don't overdo it. Just the normal endearments of an engaged couple will suffice.'

What his answer to this might have been Vera had no opportunity to find out for their 'bus was coming in sight just as they emerged from the side street. Sprinting along they caught it with no time to spare — and alighted again in the main street of Waylock Dean.

As they walked along the narrow road that led to Sunny Acres, Vera said: 'Do you think a ghost is possible?'

'I suppose anything's possible,' Dick answered. 'Even getting engaged to a pretty girl for business only is possible — '

'Dick, please be serious.'

'I think ghosts are the bunk. I have read of poltergeists and manifestations, of cheerful spooks which throw the furniture about, but I believe, seriously, that there is a mundane explanation for everything psychic.'

'That's what I think too. There must be

an explanation for what is going on in Sunny Acres. The only thing that makes me lean towards the other side is the deadly fear people seem to have of the place. I couldn't get a man to drive me to it last night.'

'Thanks,' Dick said dryly.

'I mean from the station. Don't be so — so awkward.'

He grinned and patted her hand possessively as it lay on his forearm. Then he began singing as they walked along the lonely trail towards Sunny Acres. Vera did not sing. She had too many thoughts crowding her mind. She owned Sunny Acres, and that made all the difference.

7

When they reached the castle's massive front door and hammering with the griffin knocker, Mrs. Falworth opened it to them. For a second a trace of astonishment went over her features as she saw Dick Wilmott.

'Good morning. Remember me?' he asked.

'Mr. Wilmott, I believe! The gentleman with the er — car?'

Mrs. Falworth regarded him with a composed stare, then turned her attention to Vera. The dark eyes aimed a question. Feeling well supported at last, Vera walked into the hall with a light tread, and then turned.

She said: 'I owe you an explanation, Mrs Falworth — and an apology,' she said as the woman closed the door quietly. 'Mr. Wilmott is actually my fiancé, but last night I thought I would see first what kind of a place this was before I asked him to come over and stay with me. Besides, you had not been warned of his coming and you might not have had the facilities for him to be a guest. Having seen the place, I know that everything can be easily arranged.'

Mrs. Falworth said nothing. Her hands were interlocked in front of her, her face expressionless.

'So that explains everything,' Dick added genially.

'You have not brought your car then, sir?' Mrs. Falworth asked coldly.

'That thing? Oh, no! It belongs to a friend of mine. I only borrowed it last night to run Vera over here.'

'As I recall, sir, you reside in Godalming. I heard you mention that fact to Miss Grantham last evening. How convenient that she could inherit this place, so near to you! How odd that you found it necessary to remind her of your telephone number.'

'I'd be glad if you'd have a room prepared for Mr. Wilmott,' Vera said sharply. 'He will be staying indefinitely.'

'Very well, miss.' The housekeeper

looked from one to the other of them and then asked, 'And your luggage, sir?'

'Oh, that's over in Godalming — at my friend's house. The chap who owns the car. I'll go over later and fetch it.'

Mrs. Falworth walked away and Dick said: 'She doesn't believe a word we told her.'

'Maybe not, but she can't prove anything — and you're in, which is all that counts. When we get a chance I'll show you that sealed room, but we'd better go warily in case we seem over-eager. If the dragon starts to suspect anything we may find ourselves in a mess.'

Dick followed Vera into the big drawing-room. She motioned to a chair and he sat down opposite her and held out his cigarette case.

'What I want to know,' he said, 'is what you meant by that bad smell. I've been thinking about it. What did it smell like, exactly?'

'Oh, like faulty drains, or maybe bad eggs.'

'Yet when you went through the cellar during the evening, on your first tour of inspection, you didn't notice it?'

'Not a thing, no. As far as I could tell, on my later visit, it seemed to be coming from behind the door where all the jiggery-pokery was going on.'

'And all you could see under the door was a piece of mechanism and two pairs of feet?'

'That's all. And I nearly had to stand on my head to see even that much.'

'Queer,' Dick mused, narrowing his eyes. 'And you say the dragon refused to open the door of the sealed room and as good as threatened what would happen to her husband if he tried it?'

Vera nodded. 'I did warn her, though, that I hadn't dropped the matter by any means. And I haven't. I mean to see in that room!'

'And rightly — ' Dick fell to thought for a moment, then both he and the girl looked up as Mrs Falworth entered silently.

'A room has been prepared, sir, next to Miss Grantham's. Am I to understand that you will attend to the matter of your luggage yourself?'

'That's right — and just a moment before you go, Mrs. Falworth . . . Miss Grantham has been telling me about the ghost which haunts this place. I understand that it appears once a year. When is that? At Christmas time?'

'No sir — the 21st of June, at 8.30 in the evening or thereabouts.'

Vera and Dick exchanged astonished glances and the housekeeper stood waiting, unsmiling.

'In the daylight?' Dick queried, at length.

'Obviously so, sir, since the sun does not set officially until about 10.20 summer time.'

Vera commented: 'I always thought that self-representing ghosts clanked their chains when snow cakes the ground and a bitter wind is blowing!'

'Between fiction and fact, miss, there is a lot of difference,' Mrs. Falworth remarked.

'And for how many years has this ghost been performing?' Dick demanded.

'To the best of my knowledge, sir, for the past 50 years at least. Of course I have only been here for 10 years, but I know that it has appeared on the 21st June for eight of the 10 years. There were two consecutive years when it did not manifest, maybe due to unfavourable influences — '

'Or else it lost its way,' Dick suggested, grinning.

'I am afraid, sir, that I cannot regard the manifestation of an evil spirit as — humorous.'

'Well, that depends on how you look at it . . . I suppose this spirit is that of some departed person who was wiped out in feudal times.'

'Quite the contrary, sir. The apparition takes the form of a demon — simian-eared, pointed-faced, bald, and possessing a tail. I need hardly add that a demon is an emissary of the devil, a member of his immediate retinue.'

Dick scratched his head somewhat ruefully and Vera looked as if she were fighting hard to avoid a smile.

'Is there anything further, sir?' Mrs. Falworth asked.

'How do you know what the phantom

looks like when to enter the room, according to you, means either death or the blasting of all normal reason?'

Mrs Falworth said: 'It is possible, sir, to open and close that door so rapidly that the vile influences within the room have not the time to affect you. But there is just time to see the manifestation. That has been done every year, until last year. Then Mr Merriforth took too big a risk and went right into the room to study the phantom. As I have told Miss Grantham, he emerged — or rather tottered — outside very close to madness, and for many months was desperately ill. When he did make a slow recovery he gave orders to screw up and tape the door and throw the key away. He said the door was never to be opened again.'

'That applied while he was alive,' Vera remarked, 'but now I own this house and I have decided to have that door opened this very evening.'

'I shall not help you, miss, to meet your death — or you yours, sir. Nor will my husband lend assistance.'

'All right, then, if you're so scared I'll

do it myself!' Dick said. 'Just see that a screwdriver and chisel are brought to me after dinner this evening and I'll do the rest.'

'Very well, sir,' the woman answered levelly, 'but I would urge you to reconsider.'

'One more question: What did Mr. Merriforth die of?'

'Heart failure, sir — accelerated, I believe, by his terrible experience in that room. Dr. Gillingham of Waylock Dean, who attended him during his illness, also signed the death certificate, if you require verification.'

Dick shook his head. 'That's all, Mrs Falworth, thank you.'

The woman swept out haughtily, and Dick tossed his cigarette end into the empty fireplace. Getting to his feet he began to prowl around, hands deep in his trouser pockets.

'Picked yourself a nice little legacy, didn't you?' he asked finally.

'How could I help it? It's just the way things have turned out.'

Vera rose and came over to where he

was standing. The sunlight through the ancient mullioned window misted the gold in her hair.

'You're a darned sight prettier than I'd thought,' Dick murmured, studying her.

'Will you please remember that we have a demon on our hands, Mr. Wilmott? And will you also remember that today is the 19th of June? In two more evenings the ghost will appear and that will give us a chance to see it.'

'I never thought of that!' he exclaimed, his eyes widening. 'Of course, it is the 19th today. Still, I think we ought to have a look inside that room anyway — as arranged, just to satisfy ourselves as to whether there really is a spirit of evil.'

'This evening,' Vera agreed. 'I'm game — now that I have you!'

Dick smiled and gripped her arm reassuringly.

During the afternoon Vera returned with Dick Wilmott to Godalming so that he could collect his few belongings. Apparently the mystery of Sunny Acres had got such a hold upon him that his interest in the radio store had taken second place for the time being. Either it was that or else the idea of being with Vera attracted him. She liked to think that this was the main reason.

They returned to Sunny Acres after a long, rambling walk though Godalming's beautiful countryside, arriving home just an hour before dinner was due. Old Falworth took Dick's bag upstairs without comment. Mrs. Falworth had no observations to make either. During dinner she maintained a respectful, not to say freezing, silence.

It was only when the meal had ended that she spoke.

'Am I to understand, miss, that you are still adamant in your decision to open up that room?'

'I am,' Vera assented. 'And there is nothing further to be gained by discussion. Tell your husband to fetch a chisel and screwdriver and we'll get to work right away.'

The woman hesitated, then evidently realising that further protest was useless, she turned and left the room. In a few minutes she returned and handed the chisel and screwdriver to Dick.

'Thanks,' he said briefly; then to Vera, 'Come on, dearest.'

She gave him a disapproving glance and he grinned faintly. Together they went up the stairs; then at the top they paused and looked below. They were just in time to see both Mrs. Falworth and her husband dodge back out of sight into the dining hall.

'Scared as rabbits,' Dick said. 'Okay, dearest, let's go.'

'You're overdoing it,' Vera reminded him. 'One 'dearest' per day is all I'll allow.'

'As your fiancé I insist on at least two — and we'll take up the matter of a young lover's kiss later on, shall we?'

'What!' Vera stared at him wide-eyed — then he smiled slyly and motioned along the corridor.

'Come, Miss Grantham — we have an evil aura to detect.'

They went past the evening-lit stained glass window, past the bedroom doors, to the locked chamber at the extreme end, and stood looking at the sealed door.

Somehow, downstairs, it had not seemed much of a problem to either of them to get this door open and discover what lay beyond — but now, with the memory of Mrs. Falworth's warnings and the great house quiet as a sepulchre, it seemed a different matter.

'You realize what we are risking?' Dick questioned.

'Perfectly!' Vera set her chin. 'And my mind is still made up. Go on, hurry up, before I lose my nerve.'

'Okay lady — here we go.'

He seized the screwdriver and struggled valiantly with the rusty notches in the screw heads. It was a hard task, which made him red in the face and short of breath but at least every screw was removed.

'So far, so good,' he murmured. 'Now for the rest of it.'

Then, picking up the chisel, he wedged it between the door and the frame. As he pushed hard, Vera helped him by dragging forth the wadding from round the door edges. Then suddenly, as Dick gave a shove, the lock snapped and the door

77

swung slowly inward on squeaking, rusty hinges.

Tense, motionless, they stood on the threshold and looked in. The room was completely empty. Dust lay thick and untrodden on the floor and hazed the musty atmosphere. A large stained-glass window, upon which was silhouetted the dark shadow of the 'watch tower' parapet outside, formed the one means of illumination. There was an aged fireplace, the back of which had fallen out to reveal the darkness of the flue behind it.

'Deadly, eh?' Vera asked at last, with a little sigh of relief. 'It just goes to show you what a lot of village gossip can do. Why, if it were cleaned up, this would make a nice bedroom.'

She went inside slowly, her hands on her hips, her feet making no noise in the thick dust on the carpet. It stirred up around her and into the air as she moved. Dick put down the chisel and followed her in.

'The fireplace wants fixing,' she said, as they surveyed it from the centre of the room. 'I suppose we could get somebody to attend to — '

Suddenly Vera stopped and clutched at her throat. Dick had no need to ask why she had ceased speaking, for he had noticed it at the same moment — a curious sensation, a feeling of ghastly sinking, a terrific shifting and turning of the stomach.

'I — I feel as though — I'm going to be sick . . . ' Vera got the words out in jerks, in whispers, her face deathly pale.

Dick nodded but said nothing. The lines in his face had set in a mask of strain. Both he and the girl stood still, not quite knowing what to do — but with every second, with every breath they took, they could feel inexplicable sensations creeping in upon them.

A horrible feeling crept into Dick's senses. The uncertain sunlight of the room seemed to change to a weird scrambling of shadows as intolerable pressures crushed behind his eyes.

Vera staggered. Then suddenly her knees gave way and she fell flat on the floor, face downward. Her fingers clutched vainly in the dust as she struggled to rise. Staring at her, Dick saw nameless anguish in her eyes as she looked up at him beseechingly.

With every second normalcy was deserting Dick. His brain was throbbing with horrible things that had no place in his normal make-up.

With an effort that drenched him in perspiration, he became himself for an agonising moment — but the room seemed to be filled with a myriad loathsome shapes. He bent down, caught Vera beneath her arms and dragged her out into the corridor. He slammed the door, drove home one of the screws with hands that felt numb and brittle.

Shaken, gasping for breath, tortured with a raging headache, he slumped down beside the half-conscious girl and fought to get himself under control. Gradually he began to succeed. Those unspeakable urgings began to wane as he breathed in the comparatively fresh air of the corridor. By his side Vera stirred, then at length she sat up with his supporting arm behind her shoulders.

'What happened?' she muttered, pressing a hand to her eyes.

'I — I just don't know,' Dick confessed, shaken. 'I managed to get a grip on myself for a moment or two, so I dragged you out here.'

'You are both extremely lucky to still be in possession of your lives and senses!'

Both of them looked up sharply. They had not heard Mrs Falworth's silent approach. She was standing near to them, her face inscrutable.

Dick hesitated over a remark, but instead he got to his feet and helped Vera to hers. Shaken, dusty, dishevelled, they were still breathing heavily from the experiences ... From the corridor's further distance old Falworth appeared, approaching with nervous anxiety.

'I trust you are convinced now of the evil presence within that room?' the housekeeper asked.

'I'll admit that there is something there,' Dick answered her, frowning. 'But whether it is an evil presence or not, I don't know — not yet. I haven't finished with that room by a long shot!'

'Why will you not learn sense?' Mrs Falworth sounded amazingly agitated — for her. 'If you persist in this — this baiting of the other world and its secrets, it will bring disaster down on all of us!'

'Perhaps,' Dick said, cynically. 'All I'll admit at present is that it was tough while it lasted — just like a bombing raid. Only I used to go out on a bombing raid again and again, and I'm sort of looking at that room in the same way. Just want to recover my breath, that's all — and to think things out.'

'Both of you should leave,' old Falworth put in, rubbing his hands together. 'Sell the place, Miss Grantham, and all the horror which goes with it — then we can all get away to something clean and free.'

'I probably shall,' Vera muttered, holding her aching eyes. 'For the moment I'm too dizzy to think straight. I'll go and lie down for a while.'

Dick gripped her arm as she turned uncertainly. He glanced back at Falworth.

'Take the chisel back downstairs,' he said, 'but leave the screwdriver. I'll need it to unfasten that one screw. I haven't finished the job yet — Come on, Vera.'

Still supporting her he led her down the corridor to her room, opened the door for her. Carefully he led her to an armchair and she sat down, holding her head in her hands.

'I — I suppose I shouldn't be in here,' Dick said presently, with an effort at a smile.

The girl gestured with one hand and kept her eyes closed.

'As if it mattered,' she sighed. 'Oh, my head! I feel half blind!'

8

For a few minutes Vera hardly moved. Then she began to lower her hands, and a faint, tired smile crossed her face. Dick noticed with satisfaction that color was creeping back into her cheeks, that a brightness was returning to her eyes.

'You got it worse than I did,' he said.

She said, 'I've got to sell — and quickly!'

'You say an offer has been made for this place?' Dick asked. 'Fifteen thousand pounds?'

'So Mr. Thwaite told me.'

'Any idea who made the offer?'

'Not the slightest: I didn't pursue the subject. I can't see that it matters anyway as long as we can get the money — or rather as long as I can get the money.'

'Maybe not, but it's a lot of money for a place with such a ghastly reputation.'

Vera reflected. 'The land value will be considerable, and maybe the prospective buyer doesn't want to live in it. Perhaps wants to turn the place into an institution? It would make a good one.'

Dick thought it out for a while, strolling across to the window and gazing out at the sunset. Then at length he turned and came back to the girl as she sprawled in the chair.

'You may not think much of this idea after the experience we've just been through,' he said. 'I think we should find out who is making the offer before we do anything further. I suggest that we ring up Thwaite tomorrow morning and find out . . . From a callbox, of course.'

'Well — all right — ' Vera looked up at him and gave a shrug. 'I don't suppose a day can make much difference, anyhow, but I do know when I've had enough, and this evening's experience has convinced me that there is an awful aura of evil in that locked room. You can't deny it.'

'No; I agree that it was terrible while it lasted — but I still am not converted to ghosts. Anyway, maybe we'd better talk it over in the morning when we've had a night's rest. We might as well turn in early. How do you feel?'

'I'm fine now,' Vera said, getting up. 'But I don't feel like going to sleep. My nerves are too worked up. I think I'll go down to the library and see if there are any soothing books to read.'

'I'll go with you,' Dick decided. 'I could do with a book myself and besides I don't feel any too happy at letting you out of my sight. Come on.'

Feeling almost recovered, and if anything more determined than ever to solve the mystery after their first horrifying failure, they crept out into the corridor. It was empty. Presumably the Falworths had returned to the kitchen regions again. Then Vera straightened up suddenly.

'Just why are we slinking about like a couple of fugitives?' she demanded. 'I own the place! And somebody around here is going to know it before I'm finished!'

'Atta girl!' Dick whispered, catching her arm. 'Down we go.'

They descended the staircase slowly and with dignity, but they saw no signs of the Falworths.

'Do you suppose,' Vera murmured, when they had reached the hall, 'that they think we have gone to bed and so have seized the chance to go down in the basement?'

'Maybe; but I hardly think they would risk it with the daylight still lingering. From what you have told me their activities sound like dead-of-night antics.'

Nevertheless they glanced towards the basement door inset in the staircase. It was tightly closed. Then Mrs. Falworth emerged from the passage leading to the servant's quarters. She seemed to give the faintest of starts as she saw the two at the foot of the stairs.

'I was under the impression that you had retired,' she murmured. 'I was about to lock up for the night. Will it be in order for me to do so?'

'Quite,' Vera assented briefly.

The woman inclined her head and was about to sweep towards the front door when Vera stopped her.

'Just a moment, Mrs. Falworth. I've decided on another tour of the house. My fiancé has not seen over it yet.'

'You wish to make the tour now, miss?'

'Why not? It isn't late. We'll start with the basement.'

Mrs. Falworth drew herself up. She came right to the edge of words and then checked herself. Instead she motioned towards the basement door in the side of the staircase.

'I will procure a torch, miss,' she said, and stalked away toward her own quarters. Vera watched her go and then clutched Dick's arm.

'I'm going to make her open that mystery cellar,' Vera whispered. 'That's where you will come into the picture. Insist on seeing inside it. Say it might do for dark-room photography, or something. You know.'

'All right; but watch your step. I think the dragon's dangerous!'

They waited a moment or two, then the housekeeper came back with the torch. It was spluttering. She unlocked the basement door and led the way down into the depths. In complete silence she held the torch over her head and Dick began to prowl round interestedly.

'There's a funny smell down here,' he said at length, sniffing. 'Sort of stuffy — close, as though the place wants ventilating.'

'But it seems warmer than yesterday evening when I came down,' Vera remarked. 'Wonder why?'

'I can only suggest, miss, that you were fatigued and chilled last night after your travelling,' the housekeeper said. 'I assure you that the temperature is very little different.'

'She's lying,' Vera whispered, as she prowled with Dick.

'Is this the same smell you noticed in the night?' he questioned.

'No. It's sweet violets by comparison.'

Dick raised his voice again. 'What is this queer, deadly odor, Mrs. Falworth? Any idea?'

'Perhaps the fungoid growth in the corners,' the woman answered. 'I have noticed it myself at times. Observe!'

She went over to an angle in the wall and pointed to a greenish mass flourishing in the perpetual gloom.

'Mmmm, maybe,' Dick agreed; then he

did not speak again until he came to the shattered fireplace. He stood looking down at the miscellany of bricks with the brownish red ash amongst them. It seemed to Vera that there was more ash than on her previous visit, but perhaps it was only fancy. At any rate she made no comment.

'Been burning something here, Mrs. Falworth?' Dick asked. 'It looks like linoleum ash . . . '

'Not as far as I know, sir,' she answered calmly. 'Of course I cannot answer for my husband. As the odd-job man he does quite a few things down here. He may have burned up some rubbish.'

Dick looked again at the ash, frowning; then he peered at the shattered fireplace and the black hole of the flue at the back. Finally he turned to Vera.

'Wants repairing,' he said.

Moving aside, he looked at the locked door of the neighboring cellar.

'Anything in here?' he questioned.

'Only a lot of old stuff, sir.'

'We can have that moved out. The place may be just what I want for my photographic work. Open it, please.'

The housekeeper seemed to think quickly, then realizing that the order had to be obeyed — for Vera, as mistress of the house, was nodding — she singled out a key from the small ring of them she carried and thrust it in the lock. The door opened into a dark chamber.

'If you don't mind going first, Mrs. Falworth,' Dick invited. 'You have the torch.'

Holding it high above her head, she went in. Dick followed curiously, holding on to Vera's arm. Inwardly she was tense with excitement as to what they might behold — then disappointment settled upon her instead.

There was nothing much to be seen. Against the far wall stood a very tall old bookcase with a cracked glass front. There were rolls of old linoleum, ancient chairs from which the stuffing has burst, bits of matting, bottoms from fireplaces, a rusty old coke stove — In a word, junk.

Dick raised an eyebrow at Vera and she shrugged helplessly. Where she had seen — or thought she had seen — machinery, the night before, there was now nothing but a plain flagged floor.

'Do you think it would prove suitable for a dark room, sir?' Mrs. Falworth asked Dick impassively.

'Yes — I think so. Thanks for showing it to me.'

The woman returned with them into the main cellar, locking the door behind her. Then, holding the smoky torch, she led the way up the stone steps.

'You will wish to see the servants' quarters and the other rooms, sir?'

'I don't think I'll need to bother,' Dick answered. 'I know what the bedrooms are like, and the servants' quarters don't interest me. I'll be seeing the library anyway since I'm going in to choose a book.'

'Very good, sir.' They had come to the head of the basement steps. Mrs. Falworth turned and locked the door leading to below. Her expression clearly asked if she were still needed.

Vera said, 'Thank you, Mrs. Falworth.'

The woman turned and went without a word. Dick gazed after her black-clad figure and then rubbed the back of his head.

'Didn't squeeze much juice out of that, did we?' he muttered.

'I don't understand it,' Vera declared, baffled. 'I know I saw some kind of machinery and also heard a swishing noise like water being disturbed with a stick or something.'

'Maybe you let your imagination run away with you last night. There's nothing there now, anyway.'

'But I tell you — '

'No use, darling. Can't deny the evidence of our own eyes. Let's get along to the library.'

Frowning worriedly, Vera walked with Dick to the library. He felt for his lighter.

'This oil lamp business gets on your nerves! I keep groping round for switches.'

With his lighter in flame he hunted for the lamp chandelier, found it and vaulted on to the big desk in the centre of the room. In another moment a yellow glimmer was augmenting the dying daylight through the ivy-edged windows.

'Hmmm,' he remarked. 'A lot of books here.'

'Plenty of insects, too,' Vera said, nodding to the eight specimen cases with glass tops standing on tables. 'My uncle was an entomologist and botanist, you know. Pretty famous in his way, I believe.'

Dick deserted the books to look at the specimens.

'I'm not very much up on lepidoptera myself,' he confessed, 'but there are some pretty valuable things here, obviously. The South American leaf insect, the African locust, the orthoptera of Central Asia, the South African glow-worm, the Ceylon scorpion, the South European gossamer-spider . . . Say, the old boy got around a bit, didn't he?'

Vera nodded as she also studied the cards under the specimens; then she said dryly:

'I think you're wrong with your 'lepidoptera.' Unless my memory of natural history fails me, that refers to butterflies and moths.'

'Well, never mind — insects anyway — and plants, too!' Dick added, moving to an adjoining set of showcases.

'Uncle, as I told you, was a botanist of high repute. I believe he dabbled in all sorts of flora and fauna. I seem to remember that his treatise on the heads of the western Asiatic ibexes was enough to knock your eye out. Here we have the flora.'

They studied the various odd-looking specimens. There were dried leaves, curiously shaped ferns, bits of bark, preserved brilliant-hued flowers, blades of grass that looked as though they needed a shave, and some big chunks of brownish stuff not unlike coltsfoot rock.

'Brazilian hair-leaf fern,' Dick murmured, eyeing the cards. 'Javanese oracle flower, Scandinavian xipod bark, West African pedis diaboli root . . . Your uncle must have covered half the earth, Vera!'

'He pretty nearly did,' she agreed. 'He used to vanish for months at a time. He took his insect and leaf hunting as seriously as a big game hunter does his tigers or elephants. Anyway, he was always hopping about.'

9

Dick looked again at the plant specimens, a frown crossing his face.

'Something wrong?' Vera questioned, at which he looked at her and smiled.

'No — nothing wrong. Just a passing thought . . . Now, what about the book department?'

They turned to the shelves and after a general survey they glanced at each other and registered the same reaction.

'Not so hot,' Dick sighed. 'Most of them seem to be about plants, animals or insects. Doesn't look as though your uncle went in for thrillers, Vera?'

'Don't be too sure,' she said slowly, stooping to look at several books on a lower shelf. 'There are about 20 detective stories here.'

'Evidently uncle had his lighter moments after all,' Dick decided. 'There is none here that is any good to me, though. I've read 'em all — mostly when I was in the R.A.F.'

'I've read them, too,' Vera said.

Then suddenly Dick pulled down a heavy volume.

'Say, what's this? 'The History of Sunny Acres,' including all about the legend, together with maps of the district! Looks as if it might be interesting. To judge from the dog-ears, somebody's been studying it pretty closely already.'

'Not for me, thanks,' Vera said. 'I don't want to know the history of this place. I know it too well. All I want to know, anyway!'

'Then I'll have a look at it,' Dick decided, tucking it under his arm. 'Somebody has spent a good deal of time on it so I'll do likewise.'

Vera reached out her hand at random and took down a volume. Its title made her start — Macaulay's 'Essays and Lays of Ancient Rome'.

'Wow!' Dick exclaimed. 'If you're going to read through that, I shan't see you again until next year!'

'It'll do,' she said. 'Come on.'

Dick extinguished the lamps and they

made their way slowly upstairs. In the gloom of the corridor outside Vera's rooms they stopped.

'You'll be all right?' Dick questioned.

'Of course, I'll lock my door . . . And tomorrow we'll telephone Thwaite?'

'Definitely!'

Vera waited for him to move on, but instead his hand gripped hers.

'No use taking up the matter of that engagement kiss, is there?' Dick asked.

'Not yet,' she answered calmly.

'That's what you think,' he murmured — and suddenly she felt his lips press on her cheek; then he was gone, skipping into the gloom, faintly outlined against the dim stained glass window.

'You — you fathead!' Vera breathed after him. It was not quite the right word, but it was the only one she could think of at that moment. She turned into her room with a smile on her face . . .

Much though she admired the massive prose of Macaulay, Vera found it impossible to pursue for very long his masterly exposition on Machiavelli once she got into bed. She couldn't help thinking about that kiss she had received. It took priority in her memory over the horrible events in the ghost room; it even made her forget the problem of the transformed basement below. She was almost willing to think that she had imagined things after all.

Just at this moment she was feeling comfortable for the first time since she had arrived at Sunny Acres. She was drowsily tired; a strong young man was next door ready to protect her. The sheets were cool . . . She stirred in the richness of comfort and lay on her back, head deep in the pillow, her hands locked behind it. Meditations took possession of her as she watched cool moonlight steal through the uncurtained window — meditations which trailed off into sleep.

Dick Wilmott was not asleep. He was propped up in the pillows, squinting at 'The History of Sunny Acres' and muttering uncomplimentary remarks about the dimness of the oil lamp at his side on the bed table.

He twisted and turned sharply, laid his

book flat on the bed. Stolidly he forced himself to read, not consecutively, but snatches of the close-packed context.

'It is an undoubted fact that a representative of the Devil does exist in Sunny Acres. In a long line of owners of Sunny Acres, all of them have referred to the evil presence which makes itself apparent every year on the 21st of June. There have been times, it is recorded, when it has also been seen on the 20th and 22nd of June . . . '

'Mmmm — think of that!' Dick murmured, nodding approvingly. 'Just in case it missed fire the first time, I suppose . . . '

'Whether the ghost is a genuine manifestation of the psychic realm, or whether it is the outcome of some peculiarity of the room itself is not known. Psychic experts have studied the room carefully — at times when the ghost has not been present — but they have all failed to detect the least trace of psychic phenomena.'

Dick found the lines blurring and he yawned hugely. He closed his eyes peacefully — then suddenly he sat bolt upright.

'What?' he said to himself. ' 'Failed to detect the least trace of psychic phenomena'? But what the heck! After this evening, and we were only in the room a few minutes, we were nearly laid out.' He scowled in front of him and bit the ends of his fingers, a habit from the days when he had released bombs on Berlin. 'No trace of — Vera's got to hear of this!'

He rolled out of bed and went for his dressing gown; then he slowed up and sighed, rubbed his tousled hair.

'Better not,' he muttered. 'Get back to bed, you dope!'

Disconsolate, he returned to his position between the sheets; but he was definitely awakened. The glaring fact that psychic experts had examined that room at leisure during the ghost's absence and had failed to find a thing wrong with it was full of deep significance. It meant —

'Either,' Dick whispered, 'the evil influence didn't operate in the days when this was written, or else it is a sort of induced horror! Induced? Why not? And that ties up somewhere. Something I've seen — done — felt.'

He gave it up. The notion he had drifting in the back of his mind refused to be tempted out. He looked at the book's flyleaf and found that it had been published in 1912. Still, an evil influence could hardly come on slowly. It is one of those phenomena that should have been as pungent in 1912 as it has been this very evening.

He flicked over more pages but found nothing as moving as those other few lines. Finally he scanned the index and studies the various plates referred to. One — 'Complete Map of Sunny Acres and District' — took his fancy most, but when he looked for it he got his second shock.

It was not there! The map had been torn out. Dick frowned deeply and resumed the biting of his fingernails. His mind, already jarred, had been jarred a good deal more. Of what use could the theft of a map of Sunny Acres and district be to anybody? For it had been theft. Whoever had taken it had not cut it out carefully. It had been torn out violently, hurriedly.

Dick muttered, 'There must be something in the book about it . . . '

This new angle impelled him to the book once more and he held it close under the smelly oil lamp. Between spells of heavy yawning, he read stubbornly until at last he alighted on a few relevant sentences:

'Sunny Acres — so named because from dawn to sunset some part of the house or grounds is in the sunshine — stands on the rising ground which forms the valley side of Waylock, in the trough of which lies Waylock Dean (See Plate 18 . . . listed in the Gazetteer as a hamlet). The district is rich in minerals and ancient volcanic deposits, while the atmosphere is mainly dry. It has been proven geologically that Sunny Acres has been built right across a now-sealed volcanic seam, and in consequence the grounds of the residence are richly fertile.'

'Only needs the volcano to erupt and then everybody will be happy,' Dick sighed, closing the book with a bang and relaxing wearily. 'The 'Fall of the House of Usher' wouldn't be in it! Rich in minerals and volcanic deposits, eh? See a plate that isn't there! No psychic phenomena . . . '

He forced himself to meditate for a whole, his eyes on the high ceiling. Then again an active idea took possession of him. To his way of thinking, an overcrowded mind needs a tabulated list. He took a notebook and pencil from his coat and began writing:

'No psychic phenomena. Red-brown ash in cellar. Bad smell. Volcanic deposits. Something seen somewhere which links up . . . '

He looked critically at 'Bad smell,' then crossed it out, replacing it with 'Unpleasant odor.'

'Not that I lay any claim to being a detective,' he explained to himself, as he put the note away; 'but there is something in all these incidents that forms a chain. If I could only remember the odd bit that keeps bothering me! Ah, well, I'll probably have an inspiration in time.'

Satisfied — partly at least — he blew out the lamp flame and climbed back into bed. It said much for his power of detachment that he was soon asleep.

10

If there were any disturbances in the night neither Dick nor Vera knew anything about them. They were both young, amazingly resilient, and in a way pretty pleased with themselves — so Morpheus found them willing slaves.

When they met in the morning at breakfast in the gaunt dining hall it was obvious how completely their good spirits had been restored by sleep.

'All I need,' Dick said, as he sat down at the table, 'is a good five-barred gate to jump over. And you, dearest?'

Vera, with memories of the good-night kiss, smiled sweetly.

'Never better, darling!'

'That's fine,' he approved. 'Now we're getting really chummy!'

Mrs. Falworth, as calm and unsmiling as usual, glanced at them in turn and then proceeded to her normal routine of serving the breakfast. For a while neither

Dick nor Vera spoke as they satisfied their hunger; then Mrs. Falworth broke the silence.

'With all respect, miss, might I inquire if you have made up your mind about disposing of this place? As I remember, you said last night that you would give it your consideration when you felt less fatigued.'

'I have,' Vera answered. 'Only I don't know the answer yet. It's a weighty matter — very weighty.'

It looked as though Mrs. Falworth was having a mighty hard fight to keep her patience.

'Frankly, I cannot see that the issue is so profound. You either stay and risk final obliteration by the spirit of evil or you sell and permit all of us to have our liberty.'

Vera set down her knife and fork and looked at the housekeeper with sharp blue eyes.

'Look here, Mrs. Falworth. I feel inclined to resent your implication that I am responsible for you and your husband having to stay here! You make it sound as though it is my fault that you both have to be exposed to the dangers of this evil influence just because I have not made up my mind to sell. If you wish to leave you are at perfect liberty to do so.'

'I regret, madam, that I phrased my remarks improperly. I know that you are not in any way responsible for my husband and myself staying on here — but as I said before, when I leave I wish to do so with a clear conscience. I could not give up here with the knowledge that I had left you and your — er — fiancé exposed to other-world dangers.'

'We'll take that chance if you want to quit,' Dick remarked.

Mrs. Falworth shook her head. 'I am sorry. You see, I know this house. I do not want it on my conscience that by withdrawing from it I also abandoned my protection, thereby condemning you both to insanity, or something worse. It is only my own power which holds this awful influence in check, and I do not mean that statement to sound egotistical. It is because I understand it all and can combat the evil . . . But there are limits to human endurance. I beg of you, miss — sell! Before we are all overwhelmed!'

There was a silence. Mrs. Falworth was now standing very straight, gazing upwards with her intense dark eyes, her white hands clenching and unclenching emotionally.

'Mmm — very dramatic,' Dick said.

'Will you never learn?' the woman blazed at him suddenly; then she immediately remembered herself and inclined her head towards Vera. 'Forgive me. I am not quite myself this morning. If you will excuse me I will retire for a moment and compose my emotions.'

Vera nodded somewhat blankly and watched as the tall, somber figure went from the room. Then she raised an eyebrow at Dick as he munched cheerfully.

'I'll bet she'd be a hit as Jane Eyre,' he said. 'Right down to the twiddly bits.'

'I never can make her out,' Vera said. 'I never know whether she is just acting or whether she means it. Half the time I think she is psychic and really wants to save me from disaster; and the rest of the time I think she is just a sinister woman with a diabolical turn of mind!'

'Well, either way she's darned good entertainment.'

Shaking her fair head doubtfully Vera went on with her meal. Then she asked a question.

'I suppose our plans are unchanged? We still telephone Thwaite?'

'Definitely! And we'll make a pleasant walk out of it too. I know a long walk around to a telephone box — and I'm going to tell you a lot of things while we're on our way.'

'With or without endearments?' Vera asked coolly.

'Depends. If the weather stays as hot as it is now I may come over all romantic. It's the Latin in me — But joking apart, I want serious words with you. Very serious!'

Vera could tell from his expression that he was not fooling; so she hurried through her breakfast and finished up one slice of marmalade on toast ahead of him. Then they were preparing to leave when she saw Mrs. Falworth again. Her outburst seemed to have left her more somber than ever.

'We're going out, Mrs. Falworth,' Vera informed her. 'Whether we will be back for lunch or not is not certain.'

'Very good, miss.'

She stood with her face expressionless as the two went past her to the front door. It was good to get out into the blaze of June sunshine and the soft summer breeze.

'Just like stepping out of the middle ages into the modern era,' Dick summed up.

'Plenty of relics of the middle ages in that castle I've got,' Vera sighed. 'Especially in the basement. Did you notice those rings and hooks? You should have seen the ghoulish satisfaction on the Dragon's face when she told me how they used to torture people.' She shuddered. 'What a sadistic old hag she is!'

'I noticed the — equipment, and guessed the purpose,' Dick's jaw set with uncommon firmness. 'Things haven't changed much, Vera. In those days they tore folks to pieces with red hot pliers and branding irons. In these days they rip up a fine mind — slowly, with merciless erosion. The sort of person who can do that wants acid pouring slowly down the throat . . . inside!'

'What lovely, uplifting conversation for a summer morning,' Vera murmured. They had come out of the tree-lined driveway now to the makeshift road beyond it. 'And anyway, what in the world are you talking about?'

Dick said: 'I have the most persistent thought at the back of my mind that horror can be induced! Somewhere in that castle I have seen the absolute explanation for it, but I can't think where on earth it fits in . . . That's what I wanted to talk to you about. Look — take a look at this list I made in bed last night.'

Vera took the notebook leaf he handed to her and screwed up her eyes as the sunshine reflected back from it.

' 'No psychic phenomena. Red-brown ash in cellar — ' Er, what's this? Oh! 'Unpleasant odor! Volcanic deposits. Something seen somewhere which links up — '

'I am not a detective,' Dick said, 'and I don't even pretend to be clever, but I can see that it is significant that psychic investigators for the past 50 years have examined that horror-room carefully at leisure — at leisure, mind you! And have not found a single odd thing about it!'

Vera said: 'But — ' She hesitated and moved her hand indecisively. 'This means that Uncle Cyrus and ourselves are the only ones who have experienced that sensation of being — being mentally torn apart.'

'Exactly! And we don't even know that Uncle Cyrus did have such an experience: we've only Mrs. Falworth's word for it, and that of that henpecked old rascal who's her husband. We got it good and hard, but apparently no person ever did before, except Uncle Cyrus!'

'Then what does it mean?' Vera asked helplessly.

'As I see it, one of two things. Either the evil influence came into being only recently — which to me seems absurd because an evil influence doesn't grow gradually into a full-blown aura of horror;

or else it is being created deliberately! The first time it nearly howled out old Cyrus, but not quite. He got over it, but the strain on his heart finished him not quite a year after. On the latest occasion we were attacked, but we got away with it. Not being very old we survived to tell the tale — to wonder — to suspect!'

By mutual accord they had slowed to a standstill.

Vera's face was a picture of puzzled dismay and her blue eyes were very wide.

'If the first theory is ridiculous the second isn't much better,' she said. 'How can one create horror — deliberately?'

'I admit I don't know. I've got the glimmering of an idea. It's somewhere in the house, and I saw it staring right at me! Only I can't quite fix it.'

'Most unsatisfying,' Vera sighed, walking on again with dainty footsteps. 'And I still don't think you can induce horror.'

'I'm not so sure,' Dick said. 'You can scare a sensitive child by wearing a terrifying mask; you can give it heart-failure even if you add the appropriate noises. They have a lot of fear in their make-up. The human mind is still sensitive to the unexpected: it can still recoil at the unknown and the unseen.'

Vera said: 'Between scaring a youngster by wearing a mask and having your wits blown inside out by the horror we experienced there is a world of difference! Nobody with a mask played tricks on us, Dick. We were alone. It was not hypnotism. It was sheer diabolical, soul-searing terror. Explain that — if you can!'

'I can't,' he said. 'But I do insist that if you understand the human mind well enough you can also judge how to scare it to death — literally. That's what I meant just now when I spoke of tearing a fine mind to pieces.'

'Whose mind?' Vera demanded, bewildered. 'What are you talking about?'

'Your mind, Vera. It's fine and clean. Like everything else about you. You're young and fresh, unspoiled, inexperienced enough to trust people where you ought to be suspicious of them . . . If I could prove that an attempt is afoot to break you in mind and body I'd — I'd commit murder on that person!'

'And who,' Vera asked, 'do you think is trying to do this to us? Mrs. Falworth?'

'Yes,' Dick said, his face dogged. 'I believe that frosty-faced battle-axe has the whole answer to this affair.'

For a while they walked on, then Vera gestured again:

'But Dick, why? What have I done? What did old Uncle Cyrus do? What have you done, if it comes to that? Why should such efforts be made to either destroy our sanity or kill us?'

'The idea is probably to get you out of Sunny Acres. To make you sign away ownership!'

'I thought of that long ago, but then I hit up against a brick wall. What's the point in it? If I sell the castle, the Falworths will go too; they've said so. And even if they didn't, what good would Sunny Acres be to them?'

'I don't know. There must be some purpose behind making you dissatisfied with Sunny Acres. I don't know whether it ties up with that extinct volcano over which the place is built, but it might.'

Vera's expression of wonder deepened.

'Extinct volcano? Now what? I know you've put it down on your note, and the bit about red-brown ash, but — Don't you think that it's all a bit crazy?'

'Roughly speaking, yes. There's something deadly accurate about it all when it's sorted. Another thing I can't quite swallow is why the Falworths should be so willing to carry on without wages. That doesn't make sense no matter how you look at it.'

They were silent for a while, walking through Waylock Dean's sleepy main street. Then presently Vera gave a reminiscent smile.

'Those were nice things you said about me a while ago, but I'm not half the wonder girl you seem to think. I'm quite ordinary — somewhat frightened, and very puzzled.'

'I meant what I said,' Dick answered. 'And I'm sorry I took advantage of you in the corridor last night. Put it down to masculine impulse and forget it.'

'Trouble is, I can't . . . ' Vera sounded wistful and Dick gave her a sharp glance.

She stopped walking and looked at him archly.

'I say — not here,' he protested, as she faced him, slender and appealing in the bright sunshine.

'You took advantage of the dark,' she murmured, 'and you say it was masculine impulse. I'm going to take advantage of the daylight and call it feminine impulse. Like this — !'

Dick staggered a little as her soft arms suddenly reached up around his neck and she planted her lips firmly on his. She had to stand on tip-toe to do it and it gave Ebenezer Smith, the Village's oldest inhabitant, the biggest thrill he'd had for years as he sat watching the performance from outside the cottage door.

'Quits?' Vera asked, relaxing, and she gave a pert smile.

Dick said: 'You shouldn't do such things in public!'

'Oh, go on with you!'

'When we get back to Sunny Acres,' he said, following her as she walked on again, 'I'll tie you up in that torture dungeon. You see if I don't.'

'Just as long as it's you . . . '

Dick decided he had better be quiet. The in a few minutes they reached the village post-office and both crowded into the small telephone cabinet.

'If we can ever get through to Manchester from this one-eyed dump I'll be surprised,' he said. 'What's the number?'

'I've no idea. You'll have to ask inquiry. The name's Morgan, Thwaite and Hendricks of Brazennose St., Manchester. We want Mr. Thwaite.'

Grinning, Dick picked up the telephone and so began a long verbal pilgrimage to Manchester. It was 15 minutes later and he was rather hoarse and very weary before the piping voice of an office boy floated from the industrial north.

'Mr. Thwaite, please,' Dick growled. 'And hurry it up. This is a trunk call from Surrey.'

'Wait a moment, please.'

Far beyond the three-minute call sign the voice of Thwaite replied. Immediately Dick handed the telephone to Vera.

'Hello, Mr. Thwaite!' She reached up on tip-toe to the instrument — one of those pre-flood devices perched high in the wall and made exclusively for giants. 'Vera Grantham speaking.' And she asked who had made the offer of £15,000 for Sunny Acres.

She was informed that it was Mr. Henry Carstairs, an analytical chemist of — 'Where? Of Guildford? What address? Yes — address! No, no, not something you wear — Where does he live? Ah — oh — the Nortons, Cherry Tree Rd., Guildford. Thanks, Mr. Thwaite — '

Dick wrote the address down in his notebook, the book resting on Vera's shoulder.

'How did he know is was for sale, Mr. Thwaite? Oh, he didn't? He just guessed it might be when uncle died? I see. No, I may not sell. Just considering. Yes, thanks. Goodbye!'

Vera hung the instrument up.

'Did you get it?' she asked, and Dick nodded.

11

They squeezed out of the box and went into the hot morning sunshine again.

'Well, master mind, what happens now? Nothing very extraordinary about the business, is there? Henry Carstairs knew my uncle had died and so offered £15,000 for the castle.'

'But why,' Dick mused, 'should an analytical chemist want to buy a castle, complete with ghost?'

'Don't ask me. Maybe he has ideas about an institution, or something. Anyway, I don't see what's to prevent me selling the place.'

'You've changed round a lot since you said you wanted to carry on and see what the mystery was about.'

'That was before I'd had that awful experience.'

'Well, there's nothing to prevent you from selling the place. In fact, that is probably what Henry Carstairs wants you to do — he and the Falworths.'

Vera came to a stop, frowning. She gave Dick a very direct gaze.

'Where is the connection between the Falworths and Henry Carstairs?'

'Pure deduction. The Falworths love that place so much they are prepared to stay without salary. That, to me, makes them seem suspicious. If the Falworths want you out of that place and for some reason want to buy it themselves, do you think they'd be idiots enough to try to buy it under their own name? Even granting they have £15,000 to throw about, which I doubt. They'd be more likely to get somebody else to make the bid for them — somebody with plenty of money. And I think — without proof, I admit — that Carstairs may be working in league with the Falworths. It's odd that he alone should make an offer.'

'Why is it?' Vera sounded as though she were trying to be argumentative, though to do her justice she was not. 'He lives in Guildford — quite near to you in Godalming. He must have seen the castle many a time and no doubt even knew my uncle. Probably when he heard of his death, through the local papers no doubt, he decided on an investment.'

'Unless the Falworths sent him news of the death, which accounts for him being so quick on the draw.'

'Well, all right if you want it that way. Anyhow, I feel like selling.'

Dick halted and caught the girl's hand. She halted, too, then as he motioned to the grassy bank by the side of the makeshift road to Sunny Acres she draped herself gracefully beside him.

'Look, Vera, this is really none of my business.' He looked at her with intense seriousness. 'You are perfectly entitled to do as you like with Sunny Acres, but surely you can see that if it is worth £15,000 of somebody's money it is probably worth a good deal more.'

'Must it? I'm not very good at figures.'

'Then I'll try and explain . . . ' Dick moved closer to her until he could smell the perfume wafting from her hair.

'It's a heck of a lot of money for a dump like that, even with the land round it. The evil spirit and legend alone knock about £5,000 off a price like that. I'll tell you what I think. I believe that this old castle you've inherited contains some mighty powerful money-making secret which the Falworths have stumbled upon, perhaps by accident, and they are using every means they can, short of actually killing you, to get you out! They want to uproot you legally, to make you go of your own accord. Once that is done and the property is signed away they can expand, in league with the mysterious Henry Carstairs. You see?'

'Hmmm,' Vera sat on the grassy bank and gazed reflectively at the cumulus drifting over the blue heaven. Under such conditions it was hard to dwell upon the depredations of the Falworths.

'You see?' Dick insisted.

'Yes, Dick, I see. And it would give them a nasty shock if I told them I had decided not to sell, wouldn't it?'

'It would do more than that; it would bring matters to a head in earnest. Two things might happen: either they would quit and give the whole mysterious scheme the go-by — which seems most unlikely when I recall Mrs. Falworth's dogged jaw; or else they might to the limit scare the living daylights out of you, and me, too. But if we know what's coming we'll be prepared for it.'

'Just the same, Dick, I couldn't stand another experience like the one we had in that room. I'd sooner run for my life, and I admit it.'

'And let them lick you?'

'Not them. It!'

They were quiet again, the soft breeze playing caprices with Vera's golden curls. Dick frowned into the sunny distances and then began to count on his fingers.

'One — an analytical chemist; two, queer doings in the cellar; three, castle built over an ancient volcanic seam; four, rotten smell — by gosh, I wonder!'

'Wonder what?' Vera turned lazy blue eyes towards him.

'Just an idea that's struck me, Vera, we've got to see what goes on in that cellar! The locked one, I mean. Yes, I know it looked all right when I looked over it, but that may only have been because the machinery the Falworths are using is dismantled when they've done their work. Some time or other they are bound to resume their activities down there, and when they do we must see what they're doing . . . Are you game?'

'Of course. As long as you'll stand by me, I'll stick it.'

'Right! We're going straight back to Sunny Acres and watch Mrs. Falworth's face when you tell her you're not selling.'

Mrs. Falworth, however, was too accomplished in the art of schooling her emotions to seem disturbed when Vera made her announcement during lunch. The housekeeper took the statement in absolute calm. The only change visible was slight clenching of her fingers and the creeping of a hard glitter into her dark eyes.

'I suppose, miss, it is useless for me to tell you that by your decision you have signed your own death warrant?' she asked coldly.

'Quite!' Vera answered. 'And if you wish to leave, the opportunity is still open.'

'I prefer to remain faithful to my duty, madam.'

'Do you think we are so young that we're plain crazy, Mrs. Falworth?' Dick asked her bluntly. 'You are in this castle because it suits you to be in it, and all that bunk about duty doesn't mean a thing. You are here for some vital, impelling reason, and you don't care what you do or whom you hurt so long as you make your plans work out right!'

'I am afraid, sir, I do not understand.'

Mrs. Falworth stood quite still, her smoldering eyes fixed on Dick's face.

'You will,' he promised. 'That is if you keep on behaving as you have been doing. This property is not going to be sold, and you can make up your mind to the fact that before we're finished it will have given up every secret it possesses. Every corner, every room, will be cleaned out and the myth of this legend and the evil spirit will be exploded. As a commencement we intend to resume our investigation of the horror-room this evening.'

'You have courage,' the woman admitted. 'Both of you.'

'According to my study of this place,'

Dick went on, 'from 'The History of Sunny Acres', the ghost — '

'You have read that book?' the housekeeper interrupted.

'Yes.' Dick's eyes met hers again. 'I took it out of the library last night, and I found it most interesting, not to say mysterious. One plate has been torn out — a plan of the castle and a map of the surrounding district. I presume you don't know anything about it?'

'Why should I?' But there was a definite hint of consternation in her face.

'Anyway, to go back to the ghost. It says it has been known to appear on the 20th and 22nd of June as well as on the 21st. This evening being the 20th it is a good chance to see if it proves to be accommodating.'

'I see. And if it should appear, sir, what do you intend to do?'

'Find out what makes it tick!' Dick retorted. 'There has to be a reason, and I mean to find it.'

'As you wish,' the woman shrugged; then as though there were no such things as ghosts she asked, 'Would you care for some more coffee, sir?'

Dick nodded, and glanced across at Vera. She was looking at the housekeeper intently, studying her every expression. It was quite clear that she was having a hard struggle to keep herself in check.

The lunch ended without any further exchange of words. To Vera and Dick there seemed to be nothing else on hand at the moment except another walk in the fresh air — but instead of wandering aimlessly they turned it to advantage. At 3 o'clock they called on Dr. Gillingham in Waylock Dean's main street. He was a small, composed man with a very high forehead and shrewd gray eyes. About him there hung that elusive odor of iodine and ether inseparable from a physician.

'Sorry to bother you, doctor,' Dick apologised, as Dr. Gillingham came into the waiting room in his white smock. 'It happens to be rather important though — '

'No bother at all,' Dr. Gillingham reassured him. 'These are not surgery hours, you know. What's the trouble?'

'I'm Vera Grantham,' Vera explained, as

she shook hands. 'My uncle was Cyrus Merriforth — '

'Oh, indeed! Yes, Cyrus of Sunny Acres. Quite a character, too! He mentioned you to me once or twice. Seemed to have quite a high opinion of your gallantry while in the A.T.S.'

'Oh — it was nothing . . . Suppose we forget all about me. It's my uncle I want to speak to you about. What did he die of?'

'Heart failure.'

'I suppose,' Vera ventured, 'there couldn't be any possibility of a mistake?'

'Oh!' Dr. Gillingham seemed amused. 'I value my reputation, Miss Grantham. Your uncle's heart had not been too strong for some time, dating from his unpleasant experience with the Sunny Acres' ghost.'

'That's what we want to get at,' Dick broke in. 'Miss Grantham and I are up against that phantom in earnest — or at any rate the evil power it seems to radiate. Do you think it is possible that Mr. Merriforth would still be alive but for that terrible experience he had?'

'I would say there is little doubt of it,' Dr. Gillingham answered with conviction. 'I knew him well. He came to me regularly for examination before starting on his expeditions abroad. He was a hard, sinewy man with a heart as strong as an ox's. Then one evening last summer I received an urgent call from Mrs. Falworth, his housekeeper. To my amazement I found him raving with delirium, suffering from a high fever, and his heart in a very dangerous state. We got him back to a fair state of health, but he was never quite the same man again. When I heard of his sudden death, I was not surprised.'

'What,' Vera asked, 'do you think of Mrs. Falworth?'

'I imagine that she is a most efficient housekeeper. Your uncle had nothing but praise for her. She is, I admit, a somber and forbidding person, but after 10 years in Sunny Acres one can hardly expect much else.'

'I suppose,' Dick persisted, 'Uncle Cyrus didn't call in the police after his adventure with the psychic world?'

12

Dr. Gillingham looked surprised. 'The police? What reason would he have for that? Merriforth knew that Sunny Acres possesses a ghost. He put down his own misfortune to his curiosity. No thought of police ever entered his mind.'

'A pity,' Dick said. 'You see, I believe that Mr. Merriforth was murdered! Cleverly, inhumanly — and if one can put it this way, legally. No charge could be brought against anybody because the whole plot is more or less foolproof. But I am convinced that his death was — engineered.'

Dr. Gillingham registered an expression of shocked surprise, for a moment, then he fell to thought. Finally he spoke.

'You're making a dangerous statement, Mr Wilmott, and for your own sake I shouldn't let it go any further. Sunny Acres has had a ghost for 50 years. The whole district knows about it — the simian ears, the demon's head, the curved tail — a'

'I know, but the evil influence directly responsible for the death of Merriforth never existed prior to the time he encountered it! Formerly, the ghost produced no dangerous results beyond just appearing. I believe that the terror angle is created and I am helping Miss Grantham to try to find the truth. We ourselves have just barely managed to escape a similar onslaught.'

'How very strange! Well, maybe there was some chicanery connected with Merriforth's death — I cannot say. Legally he died from heart failure, and there my responsibility ends.'

From his manner the interview was obviously at a close.

'You've been very kind doctor,' Vera said gratefully. 'We just wanted to make sure how my uncle died. Later on maybe we'll be able to tell you why he died. Thanks again.'

She shook the doctor's hand and Dick followed suit. Soon they were out in the sunlight again, walking thoughtfully along the street.

'Yes, it's clever,' Dick reflected. 'Very clever! We can't prove that your uncle was murdered, Vera, and if you or I die the same way no one could prove that to be murder either! It would all be put down to psychic phenomena.'

'I should go easy on calling it murder,' Vera said, 'until we've got some proof that the malign influence is caused by material means . . . Just what good did it do to eliminate uncle anyway?'

Dick said: 'I can only assume that the Falworths got rid of your uncle under the impression that his death would release the castle for sale if the executors of the will were agreeable. Then they discovered that you had inherited it — or maybe they knew of it already if your uncle had mentioned you to them — so they figured that you would be more concerned with selling the castle than living in it. When they found otherwise they tried to get rid of you in the same way they had got rid of your uncle.'

'Yes, it all fits in,' Vera agreed, 'even

though you seem to be taking a lot for granted. But why, Dick? What has that castle got to warrant murdering the owners?'

'That,' Dick said, 'is the problem we have to solve. But once let me get the evidence I want and I'll pay that woman Falworth out for everything! I don't forget how your brain and nerves went in that room, how you clutched at the dust in an effort to crawl out. Nobody's going to do that to you and get away with it!'

They both became quiet for a moment. In the bright sunlight of Waylock Dean, the terror of that room in Sunny Acres seemed like something of a distant world — but for a moment Dick had brought it all back in all its venomous nakedness. Through his apparent levity Vera could sense the deep, warm regard he had for her, his outraged horror at the nameless thing that had struck her down.

'You realise that we shall go with our lives in our hands again this evening don't you?' Vera asked.

'I know — but we'll not be such fools this time. A mere glimpse of the ghost is all we want. We won't go straight into the middle of the room and stand looking round. If the ghost is there this evening it will certainly be there tomorrow evening, and by then we will have devised some scheme or other . . . '

Dick broke off, laughing suddenly as they wandered along the road towards sunny Acres. Abruptly his emotions seemed to have performed an about-turn.

'To heck with the ghost!' he said. 'I'm sick and tired of it — for the moment, anyway. There are other things I want to know.'

'Such as?'

'About you, for instance. All I know about you is that you come from Manchester, own a castle with a spook, and are mighty independent. What other information have you got?'

They settled under the shadow of a giant oak and Vera said:

'My parents are dead, the blitz took care of that.'

'Oh! I'm sorry, Vera. I'm in the same boat. The Southampton air raids got my people . . . Well, anything else? Is there any genuine boy friend hanging about who is keeping me out?'

'No,' Vera answered. 'I'm quite truthful about that, Dick. You are the only boy with whom I've ever had such close acquaintance — and for a first attempt it's pretty satisfactory. I'm the kind of girl, though, who likes to weigh things up, and for that reason I prefer you on — on approbation, so to speak.'

'All right — but don't forget that it works both ways. All the time you are summing me up I'm returning the compliment. I'm not looking for an angel, because I know they don't exist — but I was looking for a girl who behaves like a girl without making an idiot of herself. Far as I can see, I've found her!'

Vera glanced at her watch and switched the conversation.

'I think it's about time we started back,' she decided. 'Just in case your feelings run away with you . . .'

Dick smiled and got to his feet, held down his hand to help her up . . .

★   ★   ★

It was nearly 5 o'clock when they reached Sunny Acres again, and they decided to stroll around the grounds. The further they moved into the unkempt jungle of weeds and massive trees the more they could appreciate Sunny Acres' imposing outline.

'All else apart, Vera, you've got a nice property here.' Dick commented, surveying the gray battlements and stained-glass windows. 'These grounds, too, properly cultivated, could be made very beautiful. I've got plenty of ideas about landscape gardening which I could turn to account.'

'You are expecting to be around a lot!' Vera murmured, slanting a provocative blue eye.

'I hope to earn the right — as the fruits of the victory we shall achieve!' Dick said. Then he ceased his banter while he studied the castle.

'Let's see now. Which is the haunted room?'

They surveyed the east wing of the great place from the driveway.

'That empty west wing takes up a good

deal of space too,' Dick mused. 'As you remarked, the place would make a first-class institution of some sort. Say isn't that the ghost room?'

He pointed up to a recess in the castle's outlines, where a massive stained-glass window lay in the shadows of the watch tower opposite to it, a parapet running round the outjutting section of stone-work. It was this watchtower, they remembered, that contained the bath-rooms.

'Yes,' Vera assented, 'that's it. And precious little it tells us. Ivy all the way up the wall and a sheer drop of about 30 feet to the drive.'

'Yes. In the shadow, too — at present. Wonder if that means anything?'

'Such as?'

'I don't know — but June 21 is the longest day in the year, and the 20th and 22nd are only slightly different. It might mean something.

Vera thought it out but arrived at no conclusion. She sighed.

'The ideas you get!' Vera said. 'After dinner we'll see if we really can discover something about that confounded room.'

They went inside and once upstairs separated to their respective rooms. When they met again in the dining hall Mrs. Falworth was present as usual, and this time she had no comments to make. What few remarks she did pass were directed entirely to matters of cuisine and nothing more. Nor did Vera or Dick give her any encouragement by indulging in vital conversation. Altogether the meal passed in uncommon quietness and the moment it was over Vera and Dick glanced at the big timepiece ticking solemnly on the heavy stone mantelshelf. It was exactly a quarter to eight.

'Time for a smoke,' Dick said, 'and then to the evening's business.'

He got up from the table and Vera did likewise. Together they strolled across the hall to the drawing room and sat down in easy chairs to enjoy their cigarettes.

'I rather think,' Dick said presently, 'that we have got the dragon on toast. She must know by now that we're on to her game, whatever it is, and she is probably racking her brains to think of a way out.'

'Or else trying to think of some way to put us out of commission more quickly,' Vera murmured. 'I don't trust a dead silence; it makes me uneasy.'

She got to her feet suddenly, as though she felt an impelling urge to keep moving.

She said: 'There is no surer way of fraying the nerves than sitting here. Let's go and get the businesses done with.'

Dick got up and followed her and just as the grandfather clock in the hall was striking 8 o'clock, they were outside the door of that deadly room once more. Propped against the frame in readiness was the screwdriver.

'We're nearly half an hour too soon,' Dick remarked, 'so let's hope the ghost will be ahead of time. We'll take a look, anyway.'

He tried to sound cheerful by whistling, then, realizing he was only being unconvincing, he gave it up and instead, applied all his energies to withdrawing the one solidly driven screw. It came out at last and a crack of light appeared down the side of the door as it swung inward slightly.

'Go on,' Vera urged. 'A flashing glimpse — no more.'

He nodded and held the doorknob tightly, leaned his body inward with arm out-thrust. The door creaked to its limit. They had time to gaze into that empty space, to note that some sunshine as pouring through one corner of the great stained-glass window — then the door had shut again.

'Whew,' Dick whispered, drawing the back of his hand across his moist forehead, 'That took a bit of nerve — like taking the fuse out of a time bomb. And there's nothing in there — no ghost — as far as I could see.'

'Not time yet, perhaps,' Vera said. 'Have to wait a bit. Did you notice any queer sensations? I didn't.'

'We were probably too quick for that.'

They waited through the most weary-ing, nerve-racking 25 minutes they had ever known. And not once during this period did either Mr. or Mrs. Falworth appear. Apparently they had decided to give up their protests and let things take their course.

'Half-past eight,' Vera said at last in a hushed voice, looking at her watch. 'Here we go!'

13

Dick opened the door again swiftly, Vera clinging to him — and they were so astounded at what they saw that he forgot for the moment to slam the door shut again.

For the phantom was there — clearly visible in the sunlight, which now blazed across the upper half of the great window. A strange, incredible caricature of a being hung in the dusty air, a haze of blurry light surrounding it from the back. There was the pointed tail, the simian ears, the long needle-chinned face, bent arms flexed as though to pounce forward. He seemed to be grinning horribly. Yet he was in mid-air and through him the ancient stone wall could be distinctly seen.

Dick slammed the door and found himself looking into Vera's dumbfounded eyes.

'Then it — it does exist,' she gasped, shocked by incredulity. 'It's not — not just a legend, after all! Look, dare we try again, just long enough to study it!'

Dick opened the door once more and they peered in on the apparition for the second time, then suddenly they began to feel the awful sensations of the previous evening. Dick slammed the door immediately, his face damp and sickly white. Firmly he drove home the imprisoning screw.

'That's enough of that,' he muttered. 'The ghost's there — but so is that awful influence. We've seen enough. Unless — ' His eyes gleamed abruptly. 'Come with me!' he said.

Vera didn't ask questions. She followed him at top speed as he raced down the staircase and into the hall. At the door leading into the basement he stopped and pulled at it. It was locked.

'Penny to a pound, if my theory is right, that the Dragon and her husband are down here,' he panted, as Vera came hurrying up to him. 'Haven't you got a duplicate key?'

'Sorry, I haven't.'

'All right — we'll wait.'

Dick stood by the door, grim-faced, then he looked around and gave a start as Mrs. Falworth appeared from the kitchen regions with vague surprise on her features.

'Oh, it is you, sir! I thought I heard somebody knocking on the front door.'

Dick looked at her blankly, then recovered himself.

'I was rattling this basement door,' he explained. 'Have you been down there at all this evening, Mrs. Falworth?'

'Why should I?' Her voice was flat and hard.

'That doesn't answer the question. Have you or not?'

'Most certainly not!'

'What about your husband?'

'He is tidying up the coke in one of the outhouses if you wish to speak to him.'

'Oh!' Dick rubbed his chin and scowled. Mrs. Falworth fixed him with her abysmal eyes for a while, then she glanced at Vera.

'Have you seen the phantom, Miss?' she inquired, her tone so off-hand she might have been referring to a visitor.

'Yes, not 10 minutes ago, and we both felt that aura of evil. But I still believe that there has got to be an explanation.'

'If you persist,' the housekeeper shrugged. 'And now, if you do not require me any further — '

Dick waved a dismissal impatiently and the woman turned and glided back towards her own domain. Vera gave Dick a puzzled look.

'You're making Mrs. Falworth decidedly suspicious. If she isn't up to anything I'm afraid she'll be resenting our attitude before very long.'

'She's up to something all right!' There was no uncertainty in Dick's statement. 'The only trouble is that I'm a bit stumped at the moment.'

'Why did you expect to find Mrs. Falworth and her husband in the cellar?'

Dick glanced around, then motioned across to the drawing-room. Once they were within it he closed the door and began to speak in a lowered voice.

'I've been doing plenty of hard thinking about this horror business, as you know — and it seems pretty obvious to me that if it isn't genuine terror-manifestation then it is a gas.'

'A gas!' Vera looked at him incredulously.

'What else can it be?' he insisted. 'It's invisible, impalpable — and we know that there are gases which can cause unconsciousness, which can deaden the nerve centers to kill severe pain, which can maim and destroy — so why not one which acts on the nerves? That would cause those awful sensations? The brain becomes deranged because of it.'

'Well, it sounds a bit wild, but granting you are right, how does it ever get into the room with nobody but ourselves present?'

'That,' Dick said, 'is the point! There is only one way — the fireplace! Is it coincidence that the back of it is knocked out so that we can see the flue behind? Is it coincidence that the back of the fireplace in the basement is also knocked out? If gas fumes were directed up from the basement fireplace they would go up between the walls and gush out again in the horror-room! That is providing there was a stoppage in the chimney. The horror-room is exactly over the basement, wall for wall, I mean. Now you can see why I expected the Falworths to be in the cellar, directing a gas up the chimney in an attempt to wipe us out when we went in that room. That they were not down there rather upsets my theory.'

'But it's a good theory!' Vera said. 'It might be possible — '

'It is possible. If only I could remember what I have at the back of my mind!' Dick said. 'I've looked right at the stuff that causes such terror, here in the house somewhere. Anyway, I'm convinced that a gas is at the back of all this horror, and that means that the Falworths engineer it.'

'And the ghost?' Vera questioned.

'Afraid I don't know.' Dick shrugged and looked at her moodily. 'It has me stumped. If it is not the genuine psychic article it is the nearest thing to it that I've ever seen. Still, one thing at a time. We want this gas problem solved first, to prove if we're right. I wonder if there are two ways to the basement? We had no chance for a proper look.' He snapped his fingers. 'Gosh, I wonder! That map of the house that I found torn out of the Sunny Acres book would show a second stairway if there is one. Maybe that is why it was removed! Just a thought, but I'll bet it isn't far wrong. The map was taken for some reason, obviously.'

They fell silent, evening gloom creeping into the room.

'It can't be the only copy of the book, surely,' Vera said. 'There might be one in the nearest public library — or Dr. Gillingham might have one, or know of one.'

'Gillingham!' Dick ejaculated, his eyes widening. 'Of course! Too late now to search for a library, but we might catch him in. Grab your hat; we're on our way.'

It was a still, warm evening outside. Without giving the forbidding house-keeper any inkling of their intentions, they hurried out, and when they reached Dr. Gillingham's home they found him off duty, with pipe in hand.

'Well, well!' He gave a welcoming smile. 'What's this time?'

'To ask a favor, doctor,' Dick answered. 'Do you happen to have a copy of a book called 'The History of Sunny Acres'?'

'Yes, I have. It's a pretty popular volume in this district. Do you want to borrow it?'

'Only for a moment, if you don't mind.'

'Keep it as long as you wish. I'll get it for you.'

With a nod he hurried out of the room, to return shortly with the book in his hand. Dick glanced at the flyleaf and noted that it was a copy of the same edition.

'Thanks, doctor. It's very good of you. I'll let you have it back in no time. Sorry to have disturbed you.'

'Not at all.' He saw them to the door and then said: 'You seem to be a most energetic young couple! Are you doing a little detective work?'

'Just that,' Dick assented. 'I believe I was right when I told you that I thought Cyrus Merriforth had been murdered . . . Incidentally, there's something that you might be able to tell me. Do you think it is possible for a gas or poisonous fumes to exist which might cause a feeling of intense horror?'

Dr. Gillingham reflected.

'Well, I wouldn't be so hasty as to deny the possibility,' he said slowly, 'but to the best of my knowledge none exists, at the moment. I admit, though, that my medical powers by no means constitute the last word.'

'But it might exist?' Dick persisted. 'It isn't a hare-brained theory?

'By no means. Human nerves are responsive to the most amazing things sometimes.'

'Well — thanks again,' Dick smiled. 'Come on, Vera; we've taken up quite enough of the doctor's time.'

He took her arm and they went down the front pathway together, Gillingham waving a genial farewell.

As they walked back along the street, Dick already peering at the book in the fast dying daylight, studying, Vera noticed, a glossy-surfaced plate intently. Then he came to an abrupt stop.

'There are two cellar exits,' he said.

Vera halted too, astonished. 'What?'

'It's right! Look here — ' He moved to the grass bank and sat down, Vera squatting at his side. He traced his finger quickly over the interior plan of the house. 'See, here is the ordinary entrance where we went down. Here's the big cellar with the fireplace and chimney clearly marked; and here's the little cellar where the queer business seems to be going on. But from that, in this corner here, there is another exit — a back-way set of stairs which come up in the kitchen regions!'

Vera snapped her fingers, her eyes bright.

'Now let's see.' Dick narrowed his eyes in reflection. 'Covering this corner when we looked into that cellar was a big old bookcase — obviously to cover the door. As for the kitchen regions, we didn't even bother to look — '

'I did, on my first night,' Vera interrupted, thinking. 'But I thought the doors I saw led to pantries and similar places. I didn't trouble to make sure. Those two could have been down there tonight and have come up that way.'

'That's just what they did do! I'm convinced of it!'

'Then how was it that on the first night I arrived they used the normal stairway?'

'Did you see them use it?' Dick questioned.

'Well, no. They were down in the cellar when I found them, and I didn't wait to see which way they came out. But the basement door was unlocked.'

'Perhaps to tempt you down, and then they never heard you.'

'Or else she forgot to lock it after our tour of inspection. I don't know. Anyway, we've got this far. What happens next?'

'We've got to scour that basement thoroughly — and the mystery basement as well — at the earliest moment, when things are propitious. Until then we — '

Dick stopped talking, peering closely at the book, at the map of the district under the plan of the castle, a map designed in geological wavy lines.

'Just look at the deposits in the district!' he cried. 'Iron ore, salt, clay, rock sulphur. All volcanic stuff and Sunny Acres is over most of them . . . That smell you noticed, was it like rotten eggs?'

'Could have been, yes.'

'Sulphur, sulphuretted hydrogen gas, anyway, smells very similar, and it's a volcanic product.'

'You don't mean that sulphur gas produces that awful sensation — ?'

'No; that's something quite different, and anyway sulphuretted hydrogen gas is too heavy to go up a flue. It floats along the ground. No, I've got another idea about the smell, and these deposits. Pretty amazing idea, too, but it might be right . . . ' He snapped the book shut. 'We have got to inspect that cellar! Now let's get back before it's too dark to see.'

14

Mrs. Falworth was just lighting the oil lamps in the hall as they re-entered the house. She glanced in their direction as they came toward her.

'You can lock up,' Vera instructed. 'We shall not be going out again. We'll have tea and biscuits and then retire.'

'Very good, miss . . . ' The housekeeper's eyes travelled to the book Dick was carrying, then she crossed to the front door and began to push across the heavy bolts.

'She saw it,' Dick murmured, as he and Vera moved into the oil-lighted drawing room. 'She must have guessed by now that we're hot-foot after her. Maybe it'll force her into the open and save us the trouble of having to sort this business out to the last detail.'

'Depends what coming into the open means,' Vera objected. 'I don't relish the thought of being killed in the middle of the night.'

'Obvious murder is not Mrs. Falworth's game. That would ruin everything for her. She prefers the gradual breaking down of a mind. That woman is a fiend at heart — as deadly as a viper — ' He broke off, patted his pockets and said, 'I wonder where my cigarettes are?'

'You had them in here last, before we went up to see the ghost,' Vera reminded him, glancing round. 'You should — There they are! Over on the table by the door.'

He got up and crossed the room. It was as he picked the case up that he gave a start and looked fixedly across the hall. The drawing room door was slightly open and he could clearly see into the yellow glow that marked the kitchen. On the wall hung an oval mirror and in it was Mrs Falworth's reflection. Dick could faintly discern her bending over two cups upon a tray, shaking something into them. It wasn't sugar, or anything of that nature. It was something in a white packet.

He turned away abruptly, fearing his own reflection might be noticed.

'Whatever you do,' he said, extending his cigarette case to Vera, 'don't drink your tea. Get rid of it somehow and pretend you have drunk it!'

'But, Dick, why on earth — ?'

'Don't drink that tea. I can't explain now. Here she comes.'

Mrs. Falworth entered a second or two later and set the try down quietly on a side table. She poured the tea into the cups and brought them across.

'That'll be all, thanks,' Vera said. 'I will ring when we have finished.'

'Very good, miss.' Mrs. Falworth went out and closed the door. Dick sniffed at his tea sharply.

'No smell,' he murmured under his breath, glancing at the door, 'but I saw her put something in these cups. I don't think she'd try to poison us. It's more likely to be a sleeping draught to keep us nice and quiet during the night. We'll pour the stuff in the fireplace. Give me your cup.'

Vera handed it over and watched as Dick emptied both cups into the huge fireplace, raking a few remaining cinders over the wet patches in the grate. Then he went over to the teapot, rinsed the cups out thoroughly with some tea in each — which again he emptied into the fireplace; then he refilled them.

'Okay now,' he said. 'Enjoy it.'

'Suppose she put some in the teapot as well?' Vera asked uneasily.

'I hardly think she would, as well as in the cups. Too much of it could kill. I'm risking it, anyway.'

So Vera risked is as well. Then they both sat quiet for 10 minutes waiting for any unusual symptoms, but nothing happened.

'We're okay,' Dick decided, relieved — still keeping his voice low. 'And incidentally, if she goes to the trouble of giving us a sleeping draught there must be something pretty important planned for tonight. It may be the chance of a lifetime for us to see what really is going on because they won't be expecting anything from us.'

'True,' Vera agreed.

'And also a chance to prove another theory,' Dick added, pondering. 'If we can be sure that they are busily engaged in the cellar we might nip back and take a look at the horror-room. If we experience no sensations of terror, that will prove conclusively that it is induced by them. And we'll be well on the way towards getting to the root of this whole business. Agreed?'

'Agreed,' Vera nodded, and they clinked empty cups to seal the bargain.

After a brief interval they put the cups on the tray and Vera rang the bell. Then she and Dick left, were halfway up the staircase as they saw the inscrutable housekeeper crossing the hall to take the tray to the kitchen.

'I'll bet she grins over those cups,' Dick murmured. 'Thinking we're going to go to sleep.'

They came to the top of the stairs in sepulchral gloom.

'Don't overdo it with light up here, do they?' Vera sighed.

'Might reveal too much of their comings and goings. Anyway, we know where our bedrooms are . . .'

They stopped outside the girl's door.

'What's the program?' she murmured.

'Well, the first essential is to stay awake; but the ideal method would be for you to sit up in my room with me; or for me to sit up in your room. Both of us just as we are, dressed and ready.'

'All right,' Vera agreed. 'Come on in.'

She could almost feel Dick staring at her. His voice sounded out of the gloom in surprise. 'I thought you'd start a lot of argument about conventions!'

'Conventions be hanged,' she said. 'I'm pretty sure by now that murder has been done and that we're next in line for it; that rubs out a lot of conventions.'

He followed her into the room, and she said: 'By the way, next time you are near a jeweller's you might get a ring and seal this business bargain of ours — '

Suddenly, in the dim gloom, she felt his arms about her.

'Vera, you're not kidding? You mean it? We've really become engaged — ?'

'I just said so,' she insisted.

Then she lit a lamp and drew the curtains.

'Queer sort of a night to get engaged, I

suppose,' she reflected.

Dick said: 'Since there may be a delay before I can get to a jeweller I think — Here! This'll show willingness, anyway!'

He drew the gold signet ring from his little finger, thrust it on the girl's third finger, left hand.

'Never did a chap meet a finer girl,' he whispered. 'You've got a lot of courage, looks — '

'And a haunted castle!' she reminded him.

'It occurs to me,' he went on, 'that I'd better hop along to my own room and lock the door from the outside in case the Falworths decide to take a peep in at me.'

He went out silently and was back in a minute with the key in his hand. He slipped it in his pocket and then motioned to chairs.

'Nothing to do now except wait for it!'

They settled themselves in easy chairs and for a while talked of commonplaces. About 11.30 they heard the Falworths come to bed.

Twelve o'clock and 1 sounded from the grandfather clock below — and finally

2. Vera was coiled up in her chair, her head pressed against the back and her eyes closed. Dick sprawled with legs outthrust and hands locked over his chest — then suddenly he drew his knees up sharply and sat listening. Reaching out he gave the girl a nudge.

'Something moving,' he whispered.

She fought the sleep out of her head and listened. To both she and Dick came the sound of feet moving softly along the corridor outside. As on that first night when Vera had listened alone, they faded presently into silence.

'On the move all right,' Vera agreed, standing up. 'Let's go.'

Dick rose and felt in his coat pocket and brought a small flashlight into view.

'I grabbed this when I went to lock my door: it may be useful. Ready?'

Vera nodded, so he turned out the dim oil lamp and then opened the bedroom door. There was the customary vista of quiet, the moon shining through the stained-glass window. Making no sounds, they went downstairs and in a few minutes reached the doorway leading to

163

the basement. It was locked.

'Might have known it,' Dick growled. 'Only one other way — take the back staircase from the kitchen. That leads right into the storage cellar and we may get a proper chance to see what they are up to. But not a sound, mind!'

Cautiously, using his flash, he led the way into the kitchen regions. The beam settled on a table, a cupboard, a cook stove, and finally on the big door in the corner. It opened at Dick's gentle touch and revealed narrow wooden stairs leading downward. A miasmic, unpleasant smell floated up to them.

'Shoes off,' Dick whispered. 'And mind the splinters.'

Vera kicked hers off and Dick untied his laces swiftly. Soundlessly they began the descent and found it ended in another door. They stood listening intently. From behind it there came that mysterious swishing of water, and borne on the air was the horrible smell. Dick sniffed at it critically.

'Very much like the residue of sulphuretted hydrogen gas,' he decided.

'And since a small percentage in the air is fatal we'd better watch our step.'

Very gently he took hold of the doorknob and turned it. The door opened ever so slightly, perhaps a quarter of an inch. Dick could feel Vera trembling with excitement as she peered over his shoulder . . .

15

A most extraordinary performance was going on beyond, and the drawback was that they dare not watch for more than a few seconds on account of the deadly odor drifting out to them.

The lumber cellar was illumined by an oil lamp, and Mr. and Mrs. Falworth were both there. The stored articles seemed to have been moved to one side. A paving stone had been raised and into the square hole it had left depended a hose. It was connected to a small hand-driven pump which old Falworth was moving up and down with surprising industry.

Scattered about the floor in various directions were bowls, bottles, and glass containers of every size and shape, some filled with water apparently, and others empty. Whatever came though the hose was sluicing out of the pump nozzle and into a large vessel like an overgrown goldfish bowl. But, most surprising thing of all, the housekeeper and her husband were both wearing respirators, not the ordinary civilian gas mask variety but laboratory masks, used exclusively for poison gas research.

'Shut — shut the door,' Vera choked, turning away. 'I — I feel sick . . . Come on!'

They floundered up the wooden steps again and back into the kitchen. In silence they put their shoes on once more.

'Well,' Vera murmured, 'what do you make of that?'

'Very interesting,' Dick's voice showed he was preoccupied. 'They're extracting water or something like it, from below. The smell is definitely that of sulphuretted hydrogen, so it does not take a Sherlock to see that they're extracting pure sulphur water.'

'Of all the cracked ideas!' Vera declared blankly.

'Cracked! Why, sweetheart, sulphur water in the pure state is one of the most valuable medicinal restoratives in existence. Ask any doctor. Take a trip to any place noted for its mineral springs and ou'll find people drinking sulphur water, and other waters rich in natural irons and other deposits. Vera, your castle is perched over a fortune!'

'It is? But what good can it do — '

'Listen, what these two scoundrels are doing with the sulphur water isn't quite clear — but apparently they are bottling it. Some of those glass vessels down there are the product of a chemical factory. If they send that stuff to a professional chemist he may add something else and sell it, quite legally, as sulphur water; or he may even extract the pure sulphur and vaporize the water, thereby leaving sulphur tablets. There are endless varieties. It means, to the Falworths and the chemist, a good income — but it does not mean the fortune that could be made if this place were turned over exclusively as a place where people came to 'take the waters'. You once said casually that this place would make a good institution. That perhaps is the very answer — a sanatorium. It would make a perfect one, with people in need of restorative coming here and taking the natural waters

— waters and chemicals mixed by the activities of a long dead volcano.'

'Whew!' Vera breathed, as the possibilities dawned on her. 'Now I understand! This could become a second Harrogate, or something — '

'Surely; and that is what the Falworths and chemist Henry Carstairs would do if only they could buy. Naturally he is the chemist who does the receiving. The tie-up is obvious. Now we begin to see why you have got to be made to give up ownership.'

'Do you think Carstairs knows the real circumstances?'

'I can't say. Perhaps he does not know what is really going on, though he must know the value of the stuff being sent to him. That is probably why he has offered £15,000 for this place, knowing he can make it many times over once he takes possession.'

Vera set her jaw. 'This settles it, Dick! I'm going to have the police in on this and get the Falworths thrown out! They've no right to do such things on my property — '

'True, but neither would you have the right either without official permission from the health ministry. I don't doubt that you would get it, but don't start a lot of things you can't finish. We have a ghost and an evil presence to solve yet and no sanatorium can ever come into being until they are eliminated. Let's keep on plodding towards a solution first . . . '

Silently they drifted out into the hall, then Vera paused.

'Why do they wear gas masks?' she asked. 'Because of the sulphuretted hydrogen gas?'

'Certainly — and it's pretty obvious that Carstairs has supplied them, since they are laboratory masks. Sulphuretted hydrogen is deadly poison. There may be other gases, too. The Falworths are taking no chances.'

'It didn't affect us much though, did it?'

'It couldn't, Dick said. 'As I mentioned before, sulphuretted hydrogen is a heavy gas. It stays close to the floor. We were probably up to our knees in it, enough of it to kill us, but all we got was a slight evil-smelling residue. Incidentally, there is a spot in America — Dead man's Gulch, I think they call it — which is part of a volcanic valley. A man can cross it, but no dog or small animal can without dying. The answer is because the gas is over the dog or small animal, but only up to a man's knees. Get the idea?'

'What beats me is how people can drink the awful stuff!'

'It undergoes certain refinements, of course, but that's a job for a professional chemist. Anyway, having solved what those two are doing our next job is to eliminate our major troubles — ghost and evil aura. Let's go up and see how things are in the ghost room . . . '

Keeping close together, they went soundlessly up the stairs and along the upper corridor, pausing finally outside the door of the horror room. Vera held the torch while Dick operated the screw-driver.

'This,' he murmured, 'is definitely the acid test! Get ready to back out quickly.'

He eased the door inward with a gentle squeak and at last he had it wide. They gazed into the dust that seemed to always cast a perpetual haze over the place. It was gloomy, illuminated — apart from the flashlight — by the moonlight. Of the demoniac phantom there was no sign.

Minutes passed, and there was not the remotest suggestion of that brain-numbing horror creeping upon them. The air smelt dusty and oppressive; nothing more.

At last Vera relaxed, her face grimly set in the torchlight.

'It begins to look as though you were right, Dick,' she murmured. 'The Falworths don't know we are in here and because of that nothing happens! That isn't just coincidence!'

They began to move into the room slowly, step by step, as though treading on quicksand; but even when they had reached the center of the chamber there was no trace of anything unusual. Finally Dick turned the flashlight toward the fireplace. Lying flat in the dust he directed the beam inside the broken back and then up the flue. Turning over, he flashed it down it. When he withdrew he was dirty but grinning in triumph.

'My guess was right, Vera!' He got up quickly. 'The upper flue of this chimney is closed with concrete or something; and the back of the fireplace having been smashed out, it seems that there is an open passage all the way down to the basement. Which also means that any fumes, gas, or smoke coming from the main cellar will float up here and, unable to escape up the chimney, will come into this room. We've got it, Vera!'

'Except that we don't know what causes the horror!'

'Yes . . . If only I could remember what it was I saw — Well, I will — in time. And now we are here let's look around for that ghost. There must be a panel in these walls or in the floor or ceiling, which might explain it. We know the outside is too sheer a drop for anything to be out there. Now, what have we?'

They began a slow prowl, Dick flashing light on every part of the stone wall, but the more they probed and examined the more evident it became that the idea of a panel was inadmissible. There could not be one in solid stone . . .

So they turned their attendance to a study of the dusty floor, smothering themselves in dirt and finishing up like two children who have had the time of their lives in an attic. But they found nothing. The floor was solid.

'Which leaves only the ceiling,' Dick decided, flashing the beam above. 'And it would be a lofty one!'

Vera said: 'Bend down and lend me your back. I'm not very heavy.'

'That's what you think!' he wheezed, as she scrambled with some difficulty on to his bent figure: 'I certainly wouldn't like to have to carry you up a mountain side!'

Vera got gradually into position, kicking off her shoes. Her hand reached down and Dick gave her the flashlight. Then, precariously balanced, she stared at the ceiling, while Dick grunted and puffed below. At her commands he staggered to different parts of the room, which she examined minutely. In fact it seemed to Dick that she was taking far longer than she needed. 'I'm not a trained acrobat, you know,' he objected finally.

'I'm not high enough,' she said. 'There's something queer clinging to this ceiling. It isn't dust; it's a sort of gray film — Boost me a few inches, can you?'

Dick straightened to the limit and then gasped in anguish as she stood on his shoulders and then on his head.

'This might be all right as a vaudeville act but to me it's a pain in the neck', he gasped. 'What are you doing, anyway?'

'Scraping some of this gray dust off into my hanky. Shan't be a moment. Down I come!'

Her feet moved back to his shoulders, then she slid down to the floor again. He took the flashlight and held the back of his neck. In the girl's outstretched hand was the little bag she had made of her handkerchief and in the center of it reposed a small quantity of powdered substance — gray with faint reddish-brown markings.

'And the idea?' Dick asked.

'Well, you seem to have ideas about gas or fumes of some sort. Either would leave a deposit. Everything like that leaves a residue. So, since there is no outlet for this hypothetical gas it must settle on the ceiling, the highest point. And it has shades in it similar to the ash in the cellar — red-brown. Maybe I've collected dust and deposit: I don't know. But if we could get the stuff analyzed we might find out something.'

A blank look had been stealing over Dick's face.

'A great idea! And I never thought of it! Very nice work, Mrs. Wilmott-to-be! Now let's get out of here before the charming Falworths think of discovering how we're going on!'

They left silently and Dick re-screwed the door. In a few minutes they were back in the girl's bedroom with the key turned in the lock.

'Point is,' Dick said, relighting the oil lamp, 'whom can we get to analyze this ash? The obvious person is Henry Carstairs — but that might mean putting our chins out too far. Just the same, it is a job for an analytical chemist.'

'I thought — perhaps Dr. Gillingham

might do it,' Vera said. 'He has helped us a lot and naturally he is interested in what is going on. I know he's not a research chemist, but he understands dispensary and all that sort of thing. He might help us.'

Dick grinned. 'Say, if you're always as bright as this in the small hours of the morning it's a pity you don't sleep in the daytime! Dr. Gillingham it is — first thing after breakfast. And if he doesn't say he's sick of seeing us on his doorstep he ought to.'

'There remains,' Vera said worriedly, 'the phantom! We are not one scrap nearer solving how it materialized into a locked room with solid walls, floor and ceiling.'

'And now is no time to think about it,' Dick decided, yawning. 'I'm going to bed and get some sleep before we start the next round. Okay?'

'Okay,' Vera agreed.

He stopped and kissed her smudged face gently as she sat holding the little bag of deposit.

'You're a great kid,' he murmured,

patting her shoulder. 'Sleep well — and see you lock your door!'

Silently he withdrew and she turned the key.

16

Their activities in the night took toll of their sleeping hours. It was half-past 10 before either of them stirred, and close on 11 when they got downstairs. In a way this was all to the good, for it looked as though a sleeping draught had done its work. On purpose, remembering that they were supposed to have been drugged, they both put on a bleary-eyed appearance as they settled at the breakfast table.

Mrs. Falworth appeared from the domestic regions after a moment or two, carrying the coffee on a tray.

'Good morning, miss — sir,' she murmured. 'I trust you slept well?'

'Too well,' Dick growled. 'Eleven hours solid is too much for anybody. Unlike me to sleep that heavily.'

'Unlike me, too,' Vera sighed. 'Maybe yesterday's fresh air.'

The edge of a tight smile appeared on Mrs. Falworth's thin lips, then she turned to the business of serving breakfast.

'I suppose, miss, you have not decided to change your mind about selling this place?' she asked presently.

'Definitely not!' I reason it this way — if it is worth £15,000 to a buyer, then it must be worth twice that and maybe more to me.'

The woman smiled gravely.

'I would remind you, madam, that today is the 21st of June, the day on which the potency of evil in this house is at maximum! I feel, in view of your continued refusal to bow to the inevitable and leave this house to the spirit that haunts it, that I must remove my beneficent influence and allow the evil power full play. In other words, I am withdrawing my protection.'

'Oh,' Vera said — not quite sure what else she should add.

'We'll survive,' Dick remarked.

'How typical of the bravado of youth!' Mrs. Falworth looked at him icily. 'I have tried by every means to show you the danger. I think that from now on you will realize that I have not exaggerated!'

More than this she refused to say, but the words gave both Vera and Dick food for thought. They were still debating them as they left the house en route to Dr. Gillingham's.

'Do you think she means to make trouble?' Vera asked. 'That is, more than she has already?'

'Only solution, I'm afraid' Dick sighed. 'Naturally she hasn't any psychic power whatsoever. The withdrawal of her non-existent protection simply means that we are going to get the works — but how violently and in what form we can't guess. Either way we're ready for her. If she goes too far we'll have to drop our efforts at detective work and turn her and her husband over to the police.'

On this decision they let the matter rest and without exchanging many more words on the way they arrived at Dr. Gillingham's about noon. To see him was impossible, the maid explained, as he had just arrived from his round of calls and was busy in the surgery. So they waited in the reception room until 1 o'clock when the doctor was at last free.

'So sorry to have kept you waiting,' he apologized as he came in. 'If it's to return the book, it could have waited.'

'It's not that, doctor,' Dick interrupted. 'I'll keep it a while yet if you don't mind. We're here to find out if you have had any experience in analysis.'

Gillingham raised his eyebrows. He raised them even more when Vera spread out her handkerchief on the table and revealed the grey and brown ash within it.

'Can you find out, by chemistry, what this is?' she asked. 'If you can it may give us the whole answer to the terror of Sunny Acres. It may even bring about a conviction for the murder of my uncle!'

Gillingham looked at the stuff closely, then sniffed at it.

'No smell,' he murmured, 'and unlike any ash I've ever seen before.'

'Can you possibly reconstruct its original nature?' Vera urged.

'Yes, I think so — providing it falls into any normal category, that is. Since so much seems to hang on it I'll have a try. Come with me.'

He led the way across the hall and into

his dispensary. He motioned to chairs, and Dick and Vera sat and watched attentively as he went through a process of chemical tests with his apparatus. But despite the thoroughness with which he worked and the various reagents he used, his disappointed face showed finally that he had failed.

'Sorry,' he said ruefully. 'It just doesn't come into any of the known basic chemicals in medicine. It simply won't react to the tests I've given it.'

He handed back the surplus ash to Vera, tightly fastened in the handkerchief. She gave Dick a disappointed look.

'You don't know anybody who might be able to help?' he prompted the doctor, who stroked his chin and reflected. Finally he seemed to make up his mind.

'There's only one man I know — or rather have heard of — who might be able to help you, and that's Carstairs of Guildford. He's a research chemist of pretty high order. Does a lot of government work in connection with the food department.'

'You mean Henry Carstairs?' Vera asked quietly.

'Yes. You know of him?'

'I — er — have heard his name mentioned,' she acknowledged, and gave Dick a meaning glance. Then she smiled. 'Well, maybe we'll try him, doctor.'

'Right. I'll look up his address for you.'

'I have it,' Vera interrupted. 'Thanks again, doctor. It's hard work solving a mystery, but we'll do it.'

They retired to the street again and looked at each other doubtfully when they were a few yards from the practitioner's gate.

'Carstairs, eh?' Dick mused. 'Now what do we do? If he is in league with the Falworths he may know what this stuff is and relay the information back to them. They will realise how far we've progressed and perhaps try to murder us in the good old-fashioned way and risk the consequences. If Carstairs doesn't know the machinations the Falworths are up to it's an even chance that he'll tell us what the stuff is.'

'Well, you don't get anywhere in this

world if you won't take a chance now and again,' Vera decided. 'I'm all for trying it. We can go from here to Guildford by bus and have lunch there — then we'll go to Carstairs' place. Might as well see what sort of a man he is, anyway.'

'You're the boss,' Dick shrugged. 'To Guildford we go.'

And they did, when the bus arrived 10 minutes later. Lunch occupied them for a further hour, then Dick consulted his notebook for the address he had written down.

'The Nortons, Cherry Tree Road,' he said. 'Right! We'll ask the cashier for directions as we go out . . . '

She told them exactly how to find their way and Cherry Tree Road proved to be highly residential and lined with somber, dusty trees.

The Nortons stood by itself, a detached house with faultlessly kept gardens and boasting a great frontage of highly polished windows. In every sense it bespoke money and house-pride.

A neat maid opened the green front door.

'Mr. Carstairs in?' Dick inquired.

'Have you an appointment, sir?'

'Well, no, but it's — '

'I'm sorry, sir, but an appointment will have to be made. Mr. Carstairs is very busy and — '

'Look here,' Vera interrupted, 'we've got to see him! It concerns a most important chemical research. Dr. Gillingham of Waylock Dean recommended us.'

The maid hesitated, then drew the door open wider and motioned into a drawing room.

'I will inquire if Mr. Carstairs can see you. Please sit down.'

Evidently, he decided that he could, for the maid came back shortly and conducted them through a side doorway across the hall, over a lawn, and so into a long, many-windowed annex at the back. Then she withdrew and left Vera and Dick in a wilderness of chemical appliances, where a tall man with upstanding black hair was brooding over a Bunsen burner.

At last he straightened up to a full six-foot-four and came forward. He had the face of an eagle — a big curved nose, powerful jaw and eyes of sharp gleaming gray. There was intelligence too, behind that lofty forehead and bald temples.

'Good afternoon,' he greeted, smiling cordially enough. 'I'm afraid I do not know your names.'

'Brixton,' Dick said quickly, with a lightning glance at Vera. 'Mr. and Mrs. Brixton. I'm a mining engineer and I've come up against a little problem which ordinary chemistry doesn't seem to touch. I happened to mention the fact to Dr. Gillingham over in Waylock Dean and he suggested I call on you.'

'Very kind of him,' Carstairs acknowledged, though whether he said it cynically or not was not entirely clear. Then he motioned to chairs. 'Sit down, won't you? Now, Mr Brixton, what's the problem?'

'One of my men has found this stuff — ' and Dick motioned to the ashy residue as Vera opened her handkerchief — 'in a test analysis of the soil near Waylock Dean. I can't decide what it is, so I wondered if you could analyze it.'

The chemist took the handkerchief Vera

held out and looked at the ash pensively, stirred it with the end of his pencil. It was hard to tell what he was thinking.

'Naturally,' Dick added, 'I'm willing to pay whatever fee there might be.'

'Only too glad to help a fellow-chemist,' Carstairs interrupted, his gaunt face breaking into a smile. 'I daresay we'll have this worked out in no time. Pardon me.'

Dick and Vera sat and watched as he went though a performance very similar to the one Gillingham had gone through. The only difference was that Carstairs seemed to be getting results. With small scoopfuls of ash shaken into different-colored liquids, and these, in turn, placed in various test tubes and heated over the Bunsen burner, he proceeded with the analysis. Finally, he had a murky sediment which he weighed in a pair of minute scales. Turning, he handed the residue in the handkerchief back to Vera, then he looked at Dick with a grim face.

'What's the idea, Mr. Brixton?' he asked shortly.

Dick gave a faint start. 'Idea? I just

want an analysis of — '

'This stuff,' Carstairs said, pointing to the scales with a bony acid-stained finger, 'is nothing more or less than pulverized granite! So fine that it has been reduced to powder, either through age or dampness. Why did you come to me to find out a thing like this? Any mining engineer or chemist should have been able to classify it immediately.'

'You are quite sure it is that?' Vera demanded.

'Positive! And now I want to know your real purpose in taking up my time. What do you both want here?'

Dick got to his feet and Vera to hers. There were danger lights in those piercing gray eyes.

'I'm sorry,' Dick apologised. 'I must have made a mistake in my reckonings somewhere. I assure you my only purpose — our only purpose — in coming here was for the analysis. How much do I owe you?'

'Only an apology,' Carstairs answered cynically. 'But since you've given that I'll say no more.'

He walked across to the door with long strides and held it open.

'The path runs round the side of the house to the front gate. Good afternoon.'

Vera and Dick did not exchange a word until they were well beyond the gate and heading for the main road.

'Whew!' Dick whistled. 'Serves us right, I suppose. Granite! Obviously dampness in the stone ceiling has made it flake and powder. And we thought — Gosh, but it's a pity! I believed we'd got on to something at last.'

'I never heard of granite dust having this coloring in it,' Vera said thoughtfully, opening her handkerchief to look at the reddish brown streaks in the gray. 'Unless an element of rust comes into it somewhere — Oh!' she finished, in blank dismay.

Dick looked at her in surprise. 'Now what?'

'I take first prize for being an idiot!' she gasped. 'No wonder he told us it is granite dust! It isn't, Dick! He knows what it is and wouldn't tell us — and here's why! Look!'

190

For a moment Dick could not understand what she meant, then he saw her initials neatly inscribed in the handkerchief's corner — V.G.

'You — you nitwit!' he exploded. 'And I told him the name was Brixton! I wonder, though, if he thought this was your maiden name initials — '

'You can be quite sure that he knows V.G. stands for Vera Grantham, and you can also be sure that he knows I'm the owner of Sunny Acres! Now we have put both feet in it with a vengeance!'

17

They returned to the castle about 5 o'clock, feeling most chastened — not to say worried, and the cold complacency of Mrs. Falworth did not help matters much. Not that she made any comments beyond inquiring if they would require dinner as usual at 7, but there was a look in her dark eyes which somehow suggested she had got everything just as she wanted it.

'Well,' Vera sighed, as she and Dick sat in the drawing room before going to change. 'We're no nearer to finding out what this ash is even now, and the way things are going we never shall be. I think we should call in the police and let the law take its course.'

'But where's our evidence?' he asked. 'We know that the Falworths dismantle their pumping equipment when they're not using that cellar, and without it in full action and them with their gas masks on we have no real proof. We can take it for granted that they keep their sulphur water samples hidden, too. As for the ghost and evil presence, the police would either laugh or else see the ghost for themselves and swear it is a genuine psychic phenomenon.'

'Then we've come to a full stop!' Vera gave a disappointed sigh. 'There's nothing more we can do!'

'Not until we find the meaning of this ash,' Dick growled. 'Oh, heck, if only I could remember . . . My mind just won't jump the gap to the answer. And it's there — waiting!'

'But surely you have some idea where you saw this — answer?'

'Not the vaguest. We did so much at first it might have been anywhere. I can't place it at all now, thought I did at the time for just a moment . . . ' Dick raised his hands and let them fall back to his knees helplessly. 'Well, Vera, we're on the last lap and we can be sure that our enemies are going to move heaven and earth to be rid of us this time! Apart from that, Mrs. Falworth said at breakfast we can reckon with Carstairs speeding things up, too, now that he knows we're on the track. And that big-nosed vulture might do anything!'

Vera said: 'And I suppose we try a little more ghost-laying tonight?'

'And the Falworths know we are going to do just that,' Dick said grimly. 'They'll turn the heat on good and proper . . . but I'm just wondering,' he finished, reflecting, 'if there might not be a way to give them the shock of their lives.'

'What?'

'Well, we enter that room and close the door — close it, mind you. They'll be watching our actions, obviously. One of them will, anyway, while the other is in the cellar, perhaps. Anyhow, after 10 minutes in the room we'll emerge again — unharmed! That ought to shake 'em! I've got a gas mask at home: one I had in the R.A.F. It should be proof against those fumes. Can you produce a mask?'

Vera gave a start. 'Why, yes! I packed it along with my things when I left Manchester. I've quite a few odds and ends out of the A.T.S. — '

'Never mind the odds and ends; it's the gas mask which counts. Dig it out while I slip home to get mine. We'll have them concealed about us somewhere when we enter that room tonight.'

Vera got to her feet hastily. 'Wait a minute! You're not going to leave me alone here while you go home. I'm coming with you.'

'All right, then — come on.'

They left the house hurriedly and saw no signs of the housekeeper as they departed. To their surprise they discovered that the weather had changed. The bright sunshine and blazing heat had given way to sullen stillness. In the far distance over the hot drowsy country-side, deep violet clouds were blowing up.

'Hmmm — thunder,' Dick sniffed. 'Typical British summer, anyway!'

They managed to cover the distance to his home and back before the storm, threatening all the time, showed signs of breaking. It was as they got into Sunny Acres at 6.15 that the first atmospheric rumblings made themselves heard.

'This is going to be lovely,' Vera commented, as they ascended the gloomy staircase. 'A thunderstorm and a ghost-hunt in gas masks, all in one evening — Whew! Give me the blitz! Incidentally, I'll examine my mask before I come down to dinner.'

Dick nodded and left her at the door of her room. The first thing she did was rummage among her belongings and bring the service mask to light. The next thing she did was change into a frock roomy enough to conceal the mask when folded. Then she tidied her hair and tried to feel composed.

It was not easy. The brooding tension before the storm was in the air. Outside the daylight had faded to a dull yellow, and the motionless trees were a harsh, unnatural green in the diffused light. Again came the rumbling of thunder, much nearer this time.

When she got to the dining hall, Vera discovered that Mrs. Falworth had lighted the oil lamps. She was standing in the uncertain light — surveying the well-laid table, when Vera came in.

'Unpleasant weather, miss,' she commented calmly.

'Oh, normal enough for our sort of summer,' Vera shrugged; then she gave a little sigh of relief as Dick put in an appearance. He took his place at the table just as a blinding flash of lightning lit the dining room. The concussion of the thunderclap on top of it made the plates vibrate.

'Mmmm — overture,' Dick commented. 'Just the right start for a nice jolly evening!'

Mrs. Falworth glided forward with the first course, then — surprisingly — she leaned gently over the table and looked at the two in turn. An unholy light seemed to be flaming in her abysmal eyes.

'Do you imagine for one moment that this storm is normal?' she whispered, her voice quivering. 'Are you such blind fools as to believe that? It is the power of evil abroad, I tell you, the power which so far I have held in check but which I have now released. It has full sway over this castle and over your unbelieving souls!'

A flash that seemed to crackle through

the windows made Vera jump transiently. For a moment all three of them were compelled to keep quiet as the thunder cannonaded.

'We're not such blind fools as you think!' Dick retorted. 'You know the whole truth about this horror business and before we're through you're going to pay for it, too!'

'You think I don't know what you have been doing?' the housekeeper snapped, straightening up again. 'Do you think I don't know that you have been running around with some ash, trying to find out if it creates horror?'

'Ah,' said Dick, 'do I detect the voice of Henry Carstairs?'

'You do! He sent a messenger over here and told me that you had been to his home under a false name and asked him to analyze some ash. It was granite deposit, as it happened. That could only have come from one place — the room! I know that because I have seen that fine deposit on the ceiling in there myself.'

'Nice of Carstairs to tell you what we

were doing!' Vera said, her cheeks red with anger.

'He did it to protect me!' Mrs. Falworth retorted, all signs of respect gone from her voice. 'He is a great friend of mine and he knows that I have psychic powers. He guessed that you were trying to prove that the evil in that room is something other than natural force and so let me have a chance to protect myself. If it did nothing else it at least assured me that you two unbelievers will have to learn through experience. For all your efforts you have not proved the horror to be anything else but psychic power, have you? For all your efforts you have found no explanation of the demon phantom!'

'We shall — in time,' Dick said steadily.

'No!' Mrs. Falworth clenched her hands in front of her and waited for a road of thunder to die away. 'No, you are too late! Tonight the powers of evil are abroad in the storm, in this castle — everywhere! It means . . . death.'

Dick shrugged as she turned away, then he looked at Vera rather uneasily as a truly appalling flash turned the windows to violet. The road and explosion of the clap seemed to shake the solid old place to its foundations.

'What's she getting at?' Vera whispered. 'Do you think she really is psychic?'

'No,' he answered curtly, slanting an eye at the woman as she busied herself at the sideboard. 'She's a clever actress, that's all, knows we have solved most of her secret and is going all out to scare us to death.'

'But Dick, this storm! It's dreadful!'

'Pretty violent, sure — but it'll pass.'

They both ate for a moment or two in silence, then Vera glanced up again.

'She's right about one thing, you know — we haven't solved the mystery of the ash or the ghost.'

'But, dearest, we do know that the influence was not there last night when she didn't know we were going in the room. That's why she's so nasty. She knows we've stolen a march on her, with that sleeping draught. There's a solution. Sure as fate.'

Dick quietened again as Mrs. Falworth drifted back to the table. Far from seeming uneasy at the savagery of the storm, she appeared to be enjoying it, as if it has something in common with her own somber, inexplicable character.

To eat under such conditions was hard work; and finally both Dick and Vera gave it up. Instead they lighted cigarettes and sat trying to compose themselves for the task now only one hour away. Perhaps the storm would clear a little in that time.

Thirty minutes later, though, the storm still raged. Mrs. Falworth had cleared the table and departed to her own regions. Dick and Vera still sat on, listening to the deluge of rain pelting on the windows and silently wishing the lightning were less vivid and the thunder less deafening.

Finally Dick got up and peered through the window. It was not a reassuring sight. The landscape was as dark as an hour after sunset with no sign of a break in the abysmal sky. Far away something red was pulsating — perhaps a building which had been struck by lightning. Then he jumped back at a sizzling flash, and a following roar exploding with it. The din ripped along and then cracked with an impact that made the deeply sunk windows rattle.

Dick said: 'It will be a bit damp for the ghost tonight, unless he wears galoshes.'

'Never in my life before have I felt so much like running for it!' Vera declared. 'Half the time I'm pretty sure that some malignant evil is abroad tonight, unless this storm happened along as a most convenient coincidence.'

Dick didn't answer for a moment. He was looking out of the window again, from where he stood. Then he shrugged.

'Lightning, I suppose. Thought I saw the headlights of a car, for a moment, coming up the drive . . . Of course the storm is a coincidence!' Dick added. 'It's the hot weather going up in noise and sizzles before a cold air current. That's all a thunderstorm is. Naturally, though, Mrs. Falworth is playing it up for all she's worth. For her it is the chance of a lifetime.'

Vera relaxed again as well as she felt able, still nursing the secret hope of an abatement in the storm. But none came. By 8.30 the onslaught seemed to have reached its peak.

'Time's up,' Dick announced, grim faced. 'Let's be off — though whether there will be ghost manifestations in this confusion I don't know.'

They went out into the hall together, their way lighted partly by the oil lamps and partly by the bewildering flashes through the windows. The great place was a bedlam of noise from swishing rain and exploding thunderclaps. Wind, too, seemed to have risen and was whistling along the upper corridor when they reached it.

Then a voice called from below. It was Mrs. Falworth's.

'For the last time, will you not be warned?'

'For the last time, no!' Dick shouted back. 'We're going in that room, and we don't believe in ghosts either!'

He caught Vera's arm and hurried her along the corridor.

'That should convince the dragon that we mean to do it,' he murmured. 'I've got my gas mask under my jacket. How about you?'

'Shan't be a moment,' Vera dodged into her room and blinked in the flashings filling the place. She was conscious of her heart racing with both excitement and alarm. She found her mask and rejoined Dick.

'Got it,' she murmured. 'Pretty bulky, I'm afraid. But she won't see anything — if she's watching — in this flickering light.'

18

They stopped outside the room and Dick quickly turned the solitary screw. Glancing sideways they saw, for a split second, the watching face of somebody at the top of the stairs — then the room was wide open before them.

'On with 'em!' Dick snapped, and they slipped the masks into place before he closed the door.

In this chamber now it was more visual terror than anything. Naked to the storm, reputed to be haunted, it presented a strain on the nerves that was well nigh unbearable. Though there was no sign of the ghost itself, and even less sign of that deadly corroding of reason, there was fear in the lightning that blazed against the mighty stained glass window, agonizing suspense in the frightful concussion of the thunderclaps.

'No ghost!' Dick mumbled behind his mask. 'I thought it would be too wet — '

Then he stopped as Vera gripped his arm. Just for an instant as the lightning flashed the ghost was there! Close to them, grinning demoniac — then it vanished again into the welter of thundering darkness. Again it hovered back as lightning ripped over the sky — and yet again — each time swimming back into blackness.

'It's there — trying to appear!' Vera's voice was hardly audible in the imprisoning rubber. 'Dick, let's get out; I can't stand any more of this — '

He turned with her to the door and for a moment raised his mask slightly. He dropped it again instantly as a wave of revulsion swept over him — but at least he had satisfied himself. The air was thickly laden with that ghastly sense of evil.

Dazzled, deafened with the thunder, they stumbled out of the room into the corridor and pulled off their masks hurriedly.

'It was there!' Vera insisted, her voice shaking. 'Momentarily, every time the lightning flashed — just as though it were struggling up out of the evil realms — '

Dick interrupted: 'It came and went with the lightning for one reason only — because it can only be seen in the light. And that,' he finished sombrely 'wants thinking about. For the moment the best thing we can do is go downstairs and see what those two are up to. They won't expect us this time.'

Holding on to each other, they sped down the lightning-drenched corridor, past the stained-glass window on which the rain was pelting in torrents, and so down the staircase. Then they came to a halt as they saw Mrs. Falworth awaiting them.

That she was shocked was plain to see. She had had the biggest surprise of her life at beholding them comparatively normal, but such was the command she held over her emotions she was impassive again almost instantly.

'Did you see the ghost?' she asked coldly.

Dick and Vera finished their descent of the stairs, the girl keeping her mask well out of sight behind her back. Dick's jacket was bulging a little, though it was unlikely Mrs. Falworth guessed the reason for it.

'Where's your husband?' Dick demanded. 'What are you waiting here for? To hear our death screams? Unlucky, aren't you? And where's your husband? Answer me!'

The woman hesitated, so Dick snapped back at her. 'All right, don't bother answering. Open that basement door!'

In silence the woman moved to it and obeyed the order.

'Get a torch and come back here — then lead the way below!'

Mrs. Falworth gave that faint, cold smile and then went into the kitchen and did exactly as she had been told. Coming back with torch in hand she led the way down the stairs. The big cellar was empty. Without hesitation Dick went over to the smashed fireplace and poked about among the broken brick-ends and discoloured ashes. Then he plunged his hands into the ash and felt about.

'Cold!' he ejaculated. 'Stone cold!'

'Might I ask, sir, what else you expected?' Mrs. Falworth inquired.

'Never mind what I expected. I was going to ask you a question upstairs — where your husband is — '

'He is in the kitchen, sir.'

'Got there by a second stairway, I suppose? Dick flared.

'Had he been down here,' the woman answered, quite composed, 'he would certainly have gone back that way. It is quicker, and the normal route for us.'

'Why did you never tell us there were two stairways down here?' Vera demanded. 'You left us to find out for ourselves!'

'I should hardly have thought the matter was of interest to you, miss. I have no wish to make a secret of the fact. You can go up them now through the storage room if you wish.'

There was a grim silence for a moment, then thunder made the ground vibrate, Mrs. Falworth's eyes narrowed a little.

'I have the right to ask what you expected to find down here!'

'Hot ash!' Dick retorted. 'Ash from the substance which creates fumes and which in turn give a feeling of horror.'

The housekeeper smiled coldly. 'So you still believe in a mundane explanation for a psychic phenomenon?'

'And for this reason . . . ' Dick faced her squarely. 'We wore gas masks in that room tonight — here's mine.' He pulled it into view and Vera revealed hers too. 'Because of that safeguard no taint in the atmosphere affected us. Evil influences are not stopped by gas masks, Mrs. Falworth!'

She was silent, her lips compressed. Then she shrugged.

'I cannot influence your theories, of course — but neither can you gainsay facts. Nothing has been burned down here tonight; that is quite evident. As for the influence not affecting you through the mask, it perhaps is not present tonight — '

'But it is! I raised my mask for a moment to see!' Dick kept his eyes fixed on the woman as he realized she was squirming mentally. 'You can't get away with it, Mrs. Falworth! You said terror would burst loose tonight and would bring death — then you turn right around and say that perhaps the influence wasn't present!'

Mrs. Falworth's face set in hard lines. 'Well, what are you going to do?'

They went up the staircase. The torch Mrs. Falworth still held sent their shadows bobbing grotesquely ahead of them. Without looking back at her, they went up to Vera's room. To their surprise there were long spells now between the flashes of lightning and resultant thunder. Nor was it as heavy.

'Clearing up,' Dick said, hurrying across to the window. 'Yes! There are breaks in the clouds to the west — even traces of sunset. I told you there was nothing psychic about it!'

Vera nodded in relief and they both sank into armchairs, visible to each other in the twilight as the storm began to clear as rapidly as it had developed.

'Well,' the girl said at least, 'you mean to send for the police?'

'No.' Dick shook his head. 'I said that because I couldn't think of anything else to say at that moment. As I told you, we want proof first — But why on earth didn't we find traces of something having been burned?'

He sat scowling in thought. Behind him a distant sheet of lightning flamed the landscape for a moment.

'What I don't see,' Vera resumed, pondering, 'is why you don't come out into the open and tell Mrs. Falworth that we both know what she and her husband are up to, with the sulphur water I mean.'

'I don't, Vera, for one very good reason. So far she does not suspect that we know about that: she has no knowledge of our excursion down below, remember. If she did know she would probably run for it after destroying all traces of the work she and her husband have been doing. That would make it next to impossible to have her — and her husband — with everything on hand when we launch the final blow.'

'She knows that we didn't take the sleeping draught, anyway,' Vera remarked. 'We couldn't have been in the ghost room otherwise.'

'Of course the stones were cold!' Dick cried, surprisingly, snapping his fingers.

'I've just been thinking ... Had the Falworths made those fumes in the normal broken down fireplace some of them would have been bound to affect them. Those respirators they have are probably not made to stand up to vapors as are service gas masks ... That means that the stuff must have been burned partly up the space between the walls — out of sight!'

'I believe,' Vera breathed, 'You may be right! Do we go and take a look, or what?'

'I think we've done enough down there for the moment. But we are going to do something — lay that ghost! Trouble is, it is not going to be easy. I want to study that horror-room from the outside, and the only way is to get out on the roof and then go down the ivy to the window ledge.'

'But what do you expect to find outside the window?' the girl asked.

'You'll see. Come on.'

He opened a window and looked outside. Everything was dripping wet and the air smelled of rain after the storm. The wind had dropped again and far to the east the lightning was still flashing at intervals. Vera moved across to where Dick was leaning out and gazed above with him.

'Uh-huh, I think it can be done,' he decided. 'I can climb to the roof by this ivy. It's tough enough to stand it.'

'Why not an extension ladder? Must be one about somewhere.'

'What! And let the Falworths know just what we're up to? Not likely! And if you want to come with me you'd better change out of that flowing frock. Anyway, here I go!'

Dick felt in his pocket for his flashlight, rid himself of his gas mask, then climbed out to the sill. Vera watched anxiously as with lithe movements he dragged himself upward in the gloom. At length his flailing legs vanished over the top of the battlements above.

'Coming?' he called down.

'Shan't be a tick — '

Vera dived back into the bedroom, changed at top speed into blouse and slacks, then launched herself out on to the ivy. It was not as difficult a task as she had expected, and by no means as bad as her service training had been. The ivy, centuries old, was enormously thick and afforded easy toe and finger holds. So finally, splashed with water from the leaves and somewhat out of breath, she scrambled over the parapet edge with Dick's hands helping her up.

'So far so good,' he murmured. 'Now follow me.'

Up there the roof was flat, but, all the same, they exercised caution in the dim light. A few yards advance brought them to facing the outjutting section of the bathrooms — otherwise the watchtower. This meant that the horror-room was now immediately below them.

'Now keep your fingers crossed,' Dick said.

He threw a leg over the battlements and started to go down, Vera watching him uneasily. Far below was the hard shale of the driveway. One flaw in that ivy meant serious injury, or death . . . Lower, Dick went, and lower, until at length he reached the sill and poised himself on it, clinging for dear life to the ivy roots. Vera waited, not in the least understanding what he was up to.

'Hello,' came his voice presently.

'What?' she asked.

'You've got to do something. Go inside the horror-room — put on your gas mask for safety — then tell me if you see the ghost.'

'But — but Dick — !' She stopped in dismay.

'You've got to do it,' he insisted. 'I can't do it for you this time. Go on — orders is orders.'

Worried, Vera withdrew from the parapet and made the return trip to her bedroom safely enough. Then she picked up her gas mask and tiptoed into the corridor, looking about her. There was no sign of the Falworths anywhere. Whether they were still downstairs or not, she had no idea.

Quickly, she unscrewed the horror-room door, slipped on her mask and stepped inside. Immediately, against the dim light of the stormy evening outside the stained glass window, she saw Dick's figure moving. Going across to it, she tapped sharply — then she jumped back in alarm as the ghost suddenly came into being — very pale and transparent, grinning, trailing a streamer of light back towards the window.

For a second or two Vera was too astonished — too horrified — to act: then forcing herself to be calm, she waved her hands in front of her. They went right through the apparition. She hesitated, uncertain what to do. Then, again, her nerve failed her and she blundered out of the room hurriedly and re-screwed the door. Slipping off her mask as she went, she hurried back into her bedroom and began the climb to the parapet. In four minutes she was peering over at Dick.

'Did you see it?' he asked.

'I should think I did — but only palely. It was there, though!'

'Then it's solved.' He gave a delighted chuckle. 'Come on down here. I'll grab you.'

19

Vera climbed over the stone edge slowly and held tenaciously to the ivy as she went down. Then to her relief Dick's arm closed round her waist and drew her in. She finished round with her feet for the broad stone ledge and stood upright a trifle dizzily.

'Okay?' Dick asked, holding her close with one arm and gripping the ivy with the other.

'If I don't look down, I am,' she answered.

'Right. Here's the ghost!'

He flashed his torch back on the window, narrowing the beam down to a small circle that finally encompassed a tiny section at the top of the big area of glass. Vera peered at it earnestly, then her brows went up in surprise. She gave a gasp of astonishment.

There, embedded in the design of the glass — which was mainly composed of diamond-shaped squares of red and green — was a tiny image, not more than four inches high and completely transparent. An image of a demon, skilfully executed as though in Indian ink on a piece of plain glass. As she passed her fingers over it and felt no roughening Vera realised that it was a picture dyed in the glass.

'So — so this is it?' she whispered at last.

'It works like a slide in a magic lantern,' Dick explained. 'I had my flashlight beam behind it when you saw it. The image is so small as to be unnoticeable in the room among all that mass of glass — and anyway, one is usually too frightened to pay close attention. But it is projected into the room by the light behind it, and the dust haze always hanging in the air acts as a kind of screen for it. Ever noticed when you're at the movies how the picture on the screen is also visible in the haze of tobacco smoke? Same sort of thing. The light which seems to surround it is actually the projected ray behind it.'

'Well, that's ingenious!'

'Several things led me to this deduction,' Dick went on, shifting his position uncomfortably. 'The first thing was that it only appears on the three longest days of the year. Now, it is right at the top of the window, and we noticed earlier — at least I did — that only that part of the window was illuminated. Those three evenings — and maybe one or two on either side of them as well — are the only ones when the sun peeps high enough over that watch tower parapet opposite to illumine this piece of glass. I mentioned the other one or two nights because the longest day really means the greatest number of solar hours. It's possible the sun peeps for about a week over that parapet there.'

'Anything else?' Vera asked excitedly.

'The fact that the phantom appeared every time lightning flashed finally convinced me. There must be a light behind it somehow. So I came out and had a look. I suppose really that the phantom would be visible in the dead of winter too, when the full moon takes the place of the sun — but that's another story. What we've done is cross off a hefty problem.

Now you'd better move. I'm getting cramp.'

Vera reached up to the ivy again and Dick helped her to get a hold. Steadily she fought her way up to the parapet above and within a few minutes he had joined her.

'Do you think,' she asked, 'that the Falworths put that piece of glass in for themselves, or has it always been there?'

'That I don't know: but I did notice that it is far cleaner that the rest of the window, so obviously they have kept it spotless inside and out to give the maximum effect . . . I'll hazard a guess — that the legend of the ghost of Sunny Acres is about as truthful as Ann Boleyn walking the Tower with her head tucked under her arm. Therefore, the Falworths decided to supply a ghost.'

'Think again,' Vera sighed. 'You told me that the history of this place stated that the ghost was known to appear on June 21st — and that book was published in 1912. So the legend can't be just bosh.'

'You're right,' Dick said. 'Well maybe

we'll get the truth later on . . . incidentally, I imagine that on the two occasions it didn't appear — according to Mrs. Falworth — the weather was probably cloudy.'

They fell silent, regarding the murky late evening. It was just starting to rain again in heavy drops.

'Well, we've progressed somewhat,' Vera decided. 'This means we have only one last problem to solve — the horror sensation. Then the coast is clear.'

'We hope . . . And we'd better get back in the house before we get drenched.'

They moved as fast as they dared along the roof through the downpour and descended the ivy again to Vera's room. Dick closed the window silently.

'I wonder,' he said, 'if Mrs. Falworth has given up trying to scare us? She vowed all sorts of things earlier in the evening but none of them seem to have materialised.'

'I think it was those gas masks that defeated her.' Vera gave a soft laugh. 'But I'll tell you what I think we should do. See where that pump hose of theirs goes and what it is really withdrawing. We might be able to get a sample of the water, and that will give the police the motive back of everything. Their chemists will soon find out what the stuff is . . . '

'Good idea . . . ' Dick lighted the oil lamp and replaced the glass chimney. He looked at the girl and smiled. 'Seems to me that we've earned a little rest after this lot! We might as well sit around for the time being, doze if we can, and then some time tonight we'll dodge down to that cellar and grab a sample — if possible. Okay?'

'Okay,' Vera agreed. And for the first time since I came here I'm not afraid of ghosts!'

For a while they both contented themselves with following their own thoughts, but subconsciously each was listening for footsteps, either denoting the Falworths coming to bed or else setting out on a nocturnal excursion.

'Be some time yet, I expect,' Dick remarked presently. 'It's only 10 o'clock — '

He broke off and sat up abruptly.

Insidiously, a feeling of horrible nausea had crept through him — and moved on. His heart began to race abruptly.

'What the — ' he began; then it cam again, surging through him. At the same moment Vera's face went deathly white in the lamplight.

'It's — it's that feeling — ' she choked.

They jumped up and stared at each other, baffled. But there was no denying it. The same awful mental revulsion of the horror-room was squirming into their senses, tearing at their nerves, battering them down —

'Can't be — in here!' Dick insisted, dry mouthed.

With a huge effort he turned as Vera swayed giddily and caught at the chair for support. Half fainting she hung there, gasping for breath. In three strides that seemed to take him through a nether world, Dick reached the window and flung it open. Rain and cool air came sweeping inwards, clearing his brain somewhat.

Dazed, he lumbered across the room and caught at the girl. His arm round her waist he dragged her, stumbling and half conscious, to the sill. She moved dully as rain pelted on the back of her neck.

Dick left her there for a moment and looked round with aching eyes. Then suddenly he remembered his gas mask and searched for it. He found it, slipped it on and drew thankfully at the purified air through the respirator. Then he began a search for Vera's, located it on the dressing table where she had tossed it, and quickly snatched it up. In 30 seconds he had it over her head. He waited beside her for a while, then she began to stir, and at last straightened up.

'Th-thanks,' she mumbled, through the folds. 'You just about saved me, I think . . . But, how did this happen?'

He looked about the room, and finally at the oil lamp. The flame was burning oddly, and with a brownish red tinge! Instantly he dived for it and using his handkerchief, took off the glass chimney. Something was visible now which he had not noticed before. On the edges of the wick holder's broad brass bands, was a residue of brownish ash still smoking and sending thin tails into the air.

'I get it!' he shouted inside his mask. 'Now I know what it is!'

He whirled the lamp up savagely and flung it clean through the open window. It went whirling down to smash and explode in a flash of burning oil on the driveway below. For a while he and Vera stood close together in the dark, waiting for the air to clear. In 10 minutes it was breathable again, though a deadly stuffiness hung upon it.

'It's the same stuffiness we noticed in the cellar the other night,' Vera said, taking off her mask and sniffing. 'You remember? It must have been surplus fumes from the stuff burning in the chimney — But you say you know what it is . . . ?'

'I remember now where I heard of it before, and where I saw it,' Dick answered. 'Come with me!'

Grabbing her arm, he whirled her out of the room, along the corridor and down the staircase. Without a pause he raced — to the girl's surprise — into the library. Muttering with impatience he lighted the oil lamps with his lighter and then hurried over to the specimen cases against the far wall.

'There!' he cried in triumph. 'Pedis Diaboli Root! That's it!'

Vera stared at the stuff, uncomprehending — two little pieces of substance like Coltsfoot rock.

'Translated it means Devil's Foot Root,' Dick explained. 'You say you've read Sherlock Holmes? Don't you remember the 'Case of the Devil's Foot'?'

'Hazily . . . ' Vera mused. 'Wasn't it something about folks who went mad — ? You don't mean that this is the same stuff?'

'No doubt of it!' Dick tapped the showcase emphatically. 'It belongs to West Africa and is known to only a few experts in toxicology. In Conan Doyle's story it was used in almost identically the same fashion as it was used on us. When heated, it gives off fumes that create violent mental derangement and leaves behind a reddish brown ash. Obviously your uncle, in his various travels abroad, found some of it and brought it back as a specimen — in fact, quite a few specimens maybe. I don't suppose he ever intended to put it to its real purpose which — according to Doyle — is that of a poison for West African natives.'

'And the Falworths knew what it was?' Vera exclaimed.

'Must have. The name card underneath is enough for any expert in toxicology — Pedis Diaboli Root. It was probably Carstairs who knew the value of the stuff. In the Sherlock Holmes story there was another Latin name added. Let's see now . . .'

Dick crossed over to the bookshelves and took down 'Sherlock Holmes, Short Stories', turned to 'The Devil's Foot.' Then, amidst the context, he pointed to three words — Rex Pedis Diaboli.

'That's it!' he cried. 'Yes, and look here! The Falworths were even unoriginal enough to use the same method as Doyle's character in that they put the stuff on the oil lamp! It was that very discovery that brought the whole thing back to my mind. I recalled a self-same incident somewhere that I'd read about . . . After that the problem was solved for me.'

20

'To think,' Vera whispered, 'that that innocent-looking stuff can create such horror when you burn it! I suppose the Falworths took some of it for themselves, and my uncle, always preoccupied, never even noticed or suspected. Tonight Mrs. Falworth must have thought that I'd be preparing for bed when the stuff began to function on the lamp. She imagined — and probably rightly — that I'd be overwhelmed before I had the chance to find out where the fumes were coming from. No wonder she has been looking so satisfied with herself! Probably there is some on your lamp as well.'

'Yes . . . ' Dick's expression was grim as he put the book back on the shelf. 'She meant making sure all right. If we didn't die in the horror-room she meant getting us afterward. It only shows you how — '

'Worked it out quite well, haven't you?' remarked a cold voice.

They both twirled in astonishment and alarm. So preoccupied had they been in fitting together the final details in the puzzle they had not heard Mrs. Falworth enter. She stood just inside the library doorway, her dark eyes malevolent, a revolver in her hand.

'I hope,' she said slowly, 'you did not think that I was going to permit you to run about the place at leisure, unmolested, poking your noses into things which do not concern you.'

Dick took an angry stride toward her but the gun jerked up menacingly.

'I wouldn't advise you to lose control of yourself, Mr Wilmott! Since every other method seems to have failed, since you have unearthed every subterfuge little by little, I am compelled to resort to straightforward means and take the consequences . . . Come here, both of you!' Then as Dick and Vera both obeyed she stood aside, still covering them, and added briefly, 'Go down into the basement!'

Dick hesitated, wondering if it would be worth his while to make a dive for the gun. Then he decided against it. Mrs. Falworth was plainly no amateur with it and if he were winged in consequence it would make matters worse than ever. So, with Vera at his side, both of them with their hands slightly raised, they crossed the hall and went down the main cellar steps. Silently, Mrs. Falworth came behind them.

Surprisingly there were two persons already in the basement — old man Falworth, grim-faced and not looking at all pleased with the proceedings, and the huge figure of Henry Carstairs. In a soft hat and heavy mackintosh from which rain had not yet dried he stood waiting in silence studying the two searchingly in the lamplight as they came forward.

'Good evening,' he murmured, bowing slightly.

Dick said, 'What do you want here?'

Carstairs smiled. 'My business will not take long, and you have really only yourselves to thank for having get into this predicament . . . That's right,' he added to Mrs. Falworth, 'keep the gun steady! My gun,' he explained, as Dick glared at him. 'I find one handy when things get — er — out of hand.'

'What,' Dick demanded, 'do you want?'

'Nothing more than Miss Grantham's signature . . .' Carstairs felt in a pocket of his coat and produced a folded square of paper complete with seals. He laid it on an upturned crate near the wall.

'That,' he explained, 'is a conveyance of this property of Sunny Acres to me. I had it drawn up this afternoon by my own lawyer the moment you two had left me. So much quicker than dealing with Morgan, Thwaite and Hendricks, don't you think? I realised that in face of what you have discovered you might not be so anxious to sell this place, Miss Grantham, and so I decided I must act swiftly and make you see reason.'

'I don't understand what you're getting at!' The girl retorted. 'Tonight both Mr. Wilmott and myself were nearly murdered. If we had died — if I had died anyway — what good would it have been to you without my signature first?'

'If you had have died, none at all,' Carstairs admitted, smiling fixedly. 'Only you wouldn't have. I am the one who prescribed the quantities of Pedis Diaboli which should be used — and each time sufficient was burned to produce raging insanity for a period with delirium afterwards, but not death . . . There is some of the stuff there,' he added, nodding to the fireplace.

Silent, Vera and Dick looked at two small sticks of substance similar to that in the library showcase.

'Yes, Miss Grantham, you would have lived,' Carstairs proceeded; 'even had you not been smart enough to wear a gas mask. You would have lived, but you would have been so broken in mind and body that you'd have been glad to sign!'

'You dirty, scheming swine!' Dick breathed, clenching his fists. 'I'll beat the hide off you for this, Carstairs! I'll — '

'And here,' the massive chemist proceeded, ignoring the outburst and holding up an oblong slip of paper, 'is my check for £15,000. Naturally I want everything to be quite legal — as indeed it must be. You have only to sign, Miss Grantham, and Mr. and Mrs. Falworth will be the witnesses. Then the property is mine and you can walk out the possessor of a small fortune.'

'And be able to tell the police about what you have done,' Vera added coldly. 'Or aren't you smart enough to have realized that? Your activities brought about the death of my uncle; therefore you murdered him — and you have attempted to murder my fiancé and me!'

'Tell the police?' Carstairs raised his eyebrows. 'And what would you tell them? That I used a rare toxic root to produce insanity? Where would be your proof? Do you think I would not destroy every trace of Pedis Diaboli the moment you had turned your back? The ghost? Well, obviously, since you have learned so much — for Mr. and Mrs. Falworth were watching your antics this evening outside the window, you know — we would take care to quickly replace the specially made demon-glass with an ordinary red one. In two moves, Miss Grantham, your — er — case for the prosecution would be wiped out!'

'He's right,' Dick growled, as the girl

looked at him helplessly. 'We wouldn't have a leg to stand on. With your name on that deed and a check for £15,000 you couldn't do a thing.'

'Exactly,' Carstairs agreed, smiling. 'You must admit that I have been very patient in trying to scare you into signing away the property. I've been most anxious to get it ever since Mr. and Mrs. Falworth found the mineral ores and water under the land. A recuperative center can be built here in Waylock Dean, and I mean to build it.'

'Would you tell me something?' Dick asked, after a pause.

'If I can,' the chemist said affably. 'What is it?'

'About that piece of glass which creates the ghost. Has it always been there or was that put there recently — to scare Uncle Cyrus?'

'The original glass contained a none too well executed demon which produced a hazy outline in the room. From that sprang the legend of the demon. When I knew the value of the land, through Mr. and Mrs. Falworth here — I decided to look into things when Mr. Merriforth was away. I solved the mystery of the ghost and had the glass replaced with a clear-cut demon outline. That, with Pedis Diaboli fumes up the chimney, was most effective. Mr. Merriforth was urged to go into the room and . . . Well, you know what happened.'

'And how do you two fit into this?' Dick asked, looking at the Falworths. 'How does it happen that you know Carstairs so well?'

'Mrs. Falworth is my sister — née Lorna Carstairs,' the chemist murmured. He relaxed a little and unbuttoned his heavy mackintosh. 'You see, Mr. Wilmott, this is not some hastily devised scheme to get money quickly — it is the work of many years of planning. I have always been ambitious. Moderate success as a research chemist and a fair amount of money left me by my father did not satisfy me. I settled in Guildford with no other idea in the world at that time than to pursue research chemistry — then in the surveyor's office one morning I happened upon some plans of the district and the value of the property here became clear to me. I had an agent ask if Mr. Merriforth would sell but I got a blunt refusal. So of course I had to try something else.'

'Then?' Dick snapped.

'I bided my time. One day I saw an advertisement for a housekeeper and handyman needed here. The former pair, I discovered later, were leaving. Anyway, I had my sister here apply for the job along with her husband — '

'I wanted none of it!' Old Falworth broke in agitatedly. 'It was my wife who insisted that we — '

'Shut up!' Carstairs told him. Then he went on, 'Well, one thing led to another. We tried all we could to make old Merriforth give up, but he wouldn't. In case he might wonder at our persistence I took the precaution, while he was away, of removing all traces of the value of this land from every book he possessed . . . '

' 'History of Sunny Acres' in particular, eh?' Dick asked.

21

'Yes, and there are others. Likewise, while he was away we made tests for mineral samples and I realized their great value. But you can only expand into real glory by turning this entire district into a spa. Finally old Merriforth came back with some Pedis Diaboli Root of all things! Quite glibly he told my sister of its awful power, and she in turn told me. I had heard of it but had never expected that such a chance would come my way. From then on, I freely admit, we worked for no other purpose than to be rid of Cyrus Merriforth. We succeeded, only to find that you came next.'

'And with my fiancé I proved too much for you,' Vera remarked, smiling coldly. 'I'm not signing anything, Mr. Carstairs, so you may as well realize it.'

'Right!' Dick agreed, nodding. 'And if you murder us in retaliation it won't do you any good. You'll never get the legal transfer that way but you will have Scotland Yard on your track mighty quick.'

Carstairs sighed and thought for a moment.

'Actually,' he said, considering, 'I was not contemplating anything so crude as murder. There are ways of persuasion, you know. As it happens we are just in the right spot to enforce that persuasion, too. I suppose you know that reluctant victims were dealt with quite thoroughly in here in medieval times?'

'Meaning what?' Vera asked, feeling herself going pale.

'Well, I could tie the pair of you up and do some root-burning from the supply by the fireplace there. Unfortunately, however, the laboratory masks are not proof against it, so that won't do. Alternatively, I could leave you bound on the floor and let sulphur gas crawl over you — only it might act so swiftly that you would die before I could get the signature . . . So I'm afraid I shall have to resort to the old-fashioned branding iron.'

'What!' Vera shrieked, taking a step back.

'You try it!' Dick clenched his fist and, regardless of the revolver, he dived for the big chemist in a flying tackle. The revolver did not explode, but Carstairs' right fist came up with savage impact and sent Dick reeling backward.

Recovering himself, he charged again, but, strong though he was, he was no match for the six-foot-four chemist. Struggling savagely, while Vera was held immovable at the point of Mrs. Falworth's revolver, he found himself slammed against the wall and his wrists imprisoned with lengths of cord fastened through the rings that hung in the stone.

'So sorry,' Carstairs apologized, stepping back finally, 'but you are a bit of a nuisance, Mr. Wilmott.' He turned to his sister and nodded. 'Fasten her up,' he said.

The woman gave Vera a vindictive shove and unable to do a thing to resist, she found herself treated exactly as Dick had been, her hands fastened to the wall rings which drew her arms out tautly on either side of her.

'Good,' Carstairs murmured, surveying both of them. 'I'm being quite lenient, you know. The old experts favored those hooks up in the ceiling there. However . . . '

He turned aside and nodded to old Falworth. Falworth hesitated, clearly not at all in favor of the proceedings, then he began to light a fire in the broken-down stonework. It took him about five minutes to get it kindled, then from a corner he took a shovelful of coke and laid it on the flames. Seizing the ancient bellows handle, he worked it up and down until the flames glowed bright red.

'You are wondering where the smoke and fumes go?' Carstairs murmured, seeing the fixed stares of Vera and Dick. 'I am afraid they go up into the ghost room since the flue is blocked. As for the root fumes, a small tin a little way up the chimney is an excellent device — All right, Tom,' he broke off. 'It's red enough now.'

The elderly man nodded, his pale eyes fixed on the core of red heat. Picking up a peculiarly fashioned iron with a long handle, he laid it in the coals. It began to heat steadily as the bellows handle went up and down squeakily.

'What are you planning?' Dick whispered hoarsely.

'Nothing that need pain you, Mr. Wilmott. You, fortunately, are valueless as a signatory. As for you, Miss Grantham, I don't think I ever knew a young lady so loath to accept £15,000. To think that I should have to burn you into taking it!'

Suddenly Carstairs dropped his easy banter, picked up the glowing iron and surveyed it. Then holding it in front of him, he advanced towards the girl. Every trace of color went from her face, but she turned toward the walls as far as her stretched arms would permit.

'Miss Grantham, if you are willing to sign that deed, you have only to nod your head.'

Carstairs' voice was pitiless, his eyes deadly. 'I promise you that I mean every word I say! I mean to have your signature.'

Vera cringed as far as she could against

the stonework. Then as, at last, she felt the heat of the iron beating on her face, across her eyes, her nerve broke.

'Wait! Wait a minute — !' The words came from her in a scream. 'I'll sign it.'

'Good!' Carstairs cried in triumph, and threw the iron back into the fire. 'Release her,' he added to his sister, who had been tensely watching.

Mrs. Falworth did as she was told, though apparently with no great enthusiasm. It seemed to Dick, watching her, as though she would have received far more satisfaction if Vera had been actually tortured.

Shaking, Vera lowered her freed arms and rubbed her wrists. Then she advanced slowly to the rough packing case upon which Carstairs had tossed the document. Calmly he unscrewed his fountain pen and handed it to her.

But before she could take it, there came an interruption. Old Falworth suddenly scooped up something from the floor and threw it in the fire.

'Get out!' he shouted. 'It's Devil's Root, on the fire — what's left of it. Get out, Miss Grantham — quick!'

Suddenly he was like a man gone mad. Twirling, he hurled himself on his wife, wrenched the gun out of her hand as she stared in amazement.

'Thought you'd get me to do as you like, didn't you?' Falworth laughed, backing towards the stairs. 'Well, now it's my turn! While you were so busy frightening this girl to death, I blocked up the space behind the fireplace with old brick-ends. The fumes can't escape upstairs. They'll come out down here! From that fire — ' The old man flashed a lightning glance at Vera. 'Get out, quick, miss!' he implored. 'Go on!'

She hesitated, but instead of obeying, she raced to Dick and began to pull on the cords fastening his wrists.

'Penknife — hip pocket,' he muttered, struggling for calmness. 'Hurry up.'

Vera dragged the knife out and snapped open the blade, slashed through the ropes. Dick dragged himself free just as Carstairs, who had made a futile effort to get near the fire, hurled himself at old Falworth. But he dodged and fired the revolver simultaneously. The chemist brought up sharp in surprised anguish, clutching his shoulder.

'You traitorous old fool!' he shouted. 'I'll kill you for this!'

Dick and Vera sped for the stairs and not a yard behind them came Falworth. Up the stone steps they went, just as the first frightful vapours came drifting out of the depths to catch them.

They reached Carstairs just as he was halfway in pursuit. He stopped suddenly, his hand moving from his shoulder to his throat. Giddily he clutched at the wall and swallowed hard. Mrs. Falworth, too, lost her iron composure and began beating at her forehead desperately, staggering about the floor.

'We — we can't leave them — !' Dick panted, perspiration wet on his face as he looked back. 'It's too horrible — '

'You're going to!' old Falworth insisted, pointing the gun. 'Keep moving!'

Unable to argue with the revolver, they crawled up the last few steps and into the fresh air of the hall. Old Falworth swung the door to and locked it. From down below came a woman's frantic scream, and the roar of a man's insane laughter.

Shaken, Vera turned away and flopped down weakly in one of the hall chairs. Silent, Dick moved to her side. Falworth remained where he was, listening, chuckling to himself at each screech of raving madness from the depths.

'Serve 'em right!' he kept muttering, shaking his head. 'They murdered!' Murdered, I tell you! Never was there a moment when I had peace with that wife of mine, or that brother of hers. Killers, both of 'em, and they died the same way as they'd planned you two should die.'

'They might come up the other staircase into the kitchen,' Dick said suddenly — but the old man shook his head and came over from the locked door.

'No, sir, they won't. They won't have the strength. They must be dead by now — and though Lorna was my wife, I say that death's too good for her. She was a fiend, and her brother was worse. I tried hard at first to tell you to get out, miss, but you wouldn't listen. Trouble was, I really meant it for your own good. After that, Lorna wouldn't let me see you, and I had to do as I was told.'

Falworth straightened up as though experiencing a vast relief. He put the revolver in his pocket. Dick and Vera looked at him with dull eyes in the dim hall light.

'We're going for the police,' he said. 'You tell them everything you've found out and I'll bear witness. They can come and look at all the evidence — the root ash, the conveyance, the check, the sulphur water — and the bodies!'

'You know what it will mean for you?' Vera asked quietly.

'Yes, miss, I know. But I'm not worrying. I was forced into what I did, and I know you two will speak for me. Now come on, will you, please?'

Dick looked at Vera steadily as she got to her feet. Then he slipped an arm round her shoulders.

'We've won, dearest,' he whispered. 'We've won! The place — with all that goes with it — is yours!'

'No — ours,' she murmured, and he hugged her tightly.

We do hope that you have enjoyed reading this large print book.

Did you know that all of our titles are available for purchase?

We publish a wide range of high quality large print books including:
Romances, Mysteries, Classics
General Fiction
Non Fiction and Westerns

Special interest titles available in large print are:
The Little Oxford Dictionary
Music Book, Song Book
Hymn Book, Service Book

Also available from us courtesy of Oxford University Press:
Young Readers' Dictionary
(large print edition)
Young Readers' Thesaurus
(large print edition)

For further information or a free brochure, please contact us at:
Ulverscroft Large Print Books Ltd.,
The Green, Bradgate Road, Anstey,
Leicester, LE7 7FU, England.
Tel: (00 44) 0116 236 4325
Fax: (00 44) 0116 234 0205

THE HARASSED HERO

Ernest Dudley

Murray Selwyn, six-foot-two and athletic, was so convinced he had not long to live that when he came across a hold-up, a murder and masses of forged fivers, he was too worried about catching a chill to give them much attention. But when he met his pretty nurse, Murray began to forget his ailments, and by the end of a breath-taking chase after some very plausible crooks, the hypochondriac had become a hero.